'A subtle, sinister coming-of-age novel ... Itani's psychological study

North Ayrshire Libraries

**This book is to be returned on or before
the last date stamped below.**

D0808846

MOST ITEMS CAN BE RENEWED BY TELEPHONE

that rare kind of writer who can make this undertow work' *Canberra Times*

Also by Frances Itani

Poached Egg on Toast (stories)
Deafening
A Season of Mourning (poems)

About the author

Frances Itani is the author of a novel, four acclaimed short story collections, three poetry collections and a children's book. She won a Commonwealth Award for *Deafening*, which was also short-listed for the 2005 International IMPAC Dublin Literary Award. Her recent collections of stories, *Poached Egg on Toast*, won the CAA Jubilee Award for Best Book of Short Stories in Canada, as well as the 2005 Ottawa Fiction Award. She grew up in Quebec, has travelled extensively, and now lives in Ottawa.

LEANING, LEANING
OVER WATER

FRANCES ITANI

Copyright © 1998 by Frances Itani

First published in Canada in 1998 by Harper Collins Publishers Ltd
First published in Great Britain in 2005 by Hodder & Stoughton
A division of Hodder Heardline

This Sceptre paperbacks edition 2006

The right of Frances Itani to be identified as the Author
of the Work has been asserted by her in accordance with the
Copyright, Designs and Patents Act 1988.

A Sceptre paperback

2

A CIP catalogue record for this book is
available from the British Library

ISBN 0 340 838647

Printed and bound by Clays Ltd, St Ives plc

Hodder Headline's policy is to use papers that are natural, renewable
and recyclable produts and made from wood grown in sustainable
forests. The logging and manufacturing processes are expected to con-
form to the environmental regulations of the country of origin

Hodder and Stoughton
A division of Hodder Headline PLC
338 Euston Road
London NW1 3BH

ACKNOWLEDGEMENTS

I wish to thank the Canada Council and the Ontario Arts Council for support during the writing of this book.

Thanks also to my friends and colleagues at Traill and Champlain colleges, Trent University, for providing retreat space when it was needed.

And I thank my mother, Frances Hill, who never flinched when I phoned day or night, asking for one more detail as I researched the forties and fifties.

The following stories have been published in slightly different versions: "A Long Narrow Bungalow" in *Canadian Fiction Magazine*; "New Year, 1953" in *The Ottawa Citizen*; "Spirit Spiders" in *Grain*; "Bolero," winner of the 1995 Tilden/CBC Literary Award, in *Saturday Night*; and "Miracles" in *Ottawa City Magazine*.

For my brothers, Terry, Brian and David.
And for our late, much-loved sister, Marilyn.

Where are you going?
... where else. To the part
that must be found out, where one day
you can return on your own.

— Armand Ruffo, "Old Story"
Opening In The Sky

The only motion or sound is that of the river,
and I do not understand that. . . . the secret will
have to be transformed into mystery before I can
understand; know.

— Rudy Wiebe,
Playing Dead

LEANING, LEANING
OVER WATER

MOVING IN

A LONG NARROW BUNGALOW

On Sunday, Maura rose an hour before she had to wake the children. She slipped through the house like a spirit, opened the front door; allowed the river breeze to filter past the screen. This was her treasured time — before she took over the grip of household affairs, before she became what she must be.

Her first sip from her cup of tea was the best moment of all. She could stand at the window to drink. She could sit on a kitchen chair. She had choices. She could take a few moments to read — not poetry, as Jock liked to do, but thick books that took months to get through because she could give them only small portions of her time. She ran her fingers over the threading cover of *Stories from Australia,* a book she deliberately read slowly because it was about far away and she wanted it to last forever.

Or she might choose not to read at all. She reached up to the shelf above the countertop and turned the knob of her radio, keeping the sound low, hoping a child would not wake and drift out of a bedroom to come and stand beside her.

The clothes for Sunday school and church were washed and ironed, ready to slip on. Eddie had polished the Sunday shoes, now lined up outside the pantry. Jock's one suit was always ready: for church, for weddings, for funerals. It hung from the coat tree behind the dining-room door. Jock's few coins were spread over the doily on the right side of the buffet. The left side was Maura's though she had nothing, really, to put there — her purse, a pair of mended gloves. This was her space — no one else's. The children were not curious and left it alone, seeing nothing of interest. But like the early morning hour that belonged to Maura, so did the rectangle of space. It was her tiny area, invisibly fenced. Maura's. Sometimes it helped her to remember who she was —

Mother, everything contained in the word. Of three children: Lyd, the eldest, with her long legs and her mother's dark hair, the one who liked to stay close to home; Trude, the watcher, neither all King nor all Meagher, the true child-between; Eddie, her only son, the earnest one who bore the curly hair of Jock's side, like the men of the King family before him.

Maura was: *Daughter.* Who'd once lived with her own widowed mother in the railroad town of Darley, Province of Ontario.

Sister, to older brother Weylin, who married Arra.

Aunt, to young Georgie, named Georgie-Porgie by her children.

And *herself:* Once a young woman who'd watched troop trains, full-bellied with cheering young men, slide past on the tracks behind her mother's house. Stood near the tracks and accepted armfuls of mail shoved at her from open windows of the trains as young men went off to war. Waited for mail of her own, mail that did not come.

She'd stood, too, in a different patch of yard, as the young men returned. A different kind of cheering, then. Lists of names in the paper in small black print; lists she'd scanned while holding her breath. Looking for names, early casualties, one name: the one who would not be coming home on those trains.

She'd met Jock during the early years of the war. Jock had stayed behind, to work in the munitions plant. He had not left; others had. Jock had not known about the other. Or the long months she'd been forced to stay inside, or the hidden loss at the end.

Maura tried not to think, tried not to remember.

She had become —

Wife. Of Jock King, who several years after the war, when the converted plant was about to shut down, hauled an atlas from the shelf and was seduced by the horseshoe shape of the Canadian Shield. "The earth in its most solid state," he told her. "Bare-bones Precambrian rock." Maura was not so sure. The speck of village from which he'd returned and announced that he'd found a job was on the edge of a wide river. In the atlas, the speck was borderline, definitely borderline. "Wait till you see the view," Jock had told her. "You could travel to Kingdom Come and back, and you'd never see a view like this."

And brought her, on a train, with three children. First to Ottawa, where they transferred to a streetcar that carried them across the river to Quebec. Then, a bus, the whole trip taking an hour and a half to reach —

House. A long narrow bungalow in a tiny village at the end of a dirt road beside the swiftest portion of the Ottawa River. That first day when Maura had stood inside the closed front porch and looked out at heaving rapids through its many windows, Jock had come up behind her and said, "We're on the edge but we made it. I think we're okay." He'd tapped a foot on the porch floor as if to let her know that the house itself might be constructed of Precambrian rock. Though Jock was inches away, he did not reach through the space between them. Maura looked down at the painted grey boards of the porch floor and out across the water towards Ontario. She thought of the darkness she'd left behind; she tried not to be pulled back by sorrow. But all she could say to herself was: *He's brought me to live beside a fast-flowing river, and I don't know how to swim.*

Now, on this Sunday morning, moments before she tiptoed into the bedrooms to wake the children, she became aware of the lulling sound of choral music that drifted from the radio above her. She felt herself rise to meet it, an expanse of her that rushed through the house and out the door and into the world beyond.

Jock lay in bed, listening for the all-clear. He pictured his wife and children running through the field to catch the bus out of the village and he murmured to himself, "The whole creation groaneth and travaileth." He had no particular duties that day and did not have to join his family in Hull, later, for church. He would listen to "Sunday Chorale" on CBC, in the evening, instead. For now, he just wanted to lie there, thinking or not thinking. Sunday morning was the only time he ever got to be alone in his own home.

He closed his eyes and waited for the silence to open. Heard the late summer call of the killdeer and was thankful for the mercy of Sundays. Thankful that he did not have to get up at daybreak and walk the length of the village, his soles grinding into cinder chips as he neared the factory. Thankful that he did not have to listen to the enduring drone and slap of machine, or fill orders in August for the Christmas market in Saskatchewan, windows propped open with sticks all around him, men working in their undershirts, no place to escape the heat; the long open room of stone as good as it was going to get. He did not have to lean into the wide sill where he stood to eat his lunch. Nor look through the open window, wondering at the ability of buttercup and thistle to erupt through stone. No, he lay on his mattress and sank into his day of rest. Listened to the shore birds, and allowed words to ripple through his head. He reached for the book of poems on his bedside table, but before he opened the cover, his memory released part of its hoard — lines of a poet who once sat at a desk on this same continent and wrote:

My lady's hair the fond winds stir
And all the birds make songs for her.

Jock thought of how he had left Darley. Of jobs he'd had and jobs that were still to come. "Set me down anywhere and I can adapt," he'd told Maura. "I can adapt to anything." It was his picture of himself, meeting change and adversity. In his last job, before they'd moved, he'd known that the plant would close. Town going under, he'd told Maura. Through silent resistance, he'd said to himself: *Dead-end town.* He had a family to feed.

On weekends he boarded buses, riding to nearby places to scout around for work, interesting work, not munitions work. The trips took him farther and farther. He quit the buses because choking dust rose up through the floors.

He switched to trains, the longest journey taking him east, to Ottawa. Before he stepped down and into the grand spaces of Union Station, the train hauled him across a trestle spanning the Ottawa River. Past the E. B. Eddy mills and up over the old timber slides at the Chaudière Falls. Minutes later, after poking its engine into Hull, the train recrossed the river on a high soot-blackened bridge and chuffed back to Ottawa. Jock looked over his shoulder at pyramids of logs taller than the buildings of the mill itself. What he saw was Quebec.

Any place that has this much timber has a job for me, he said. His footsteps echoed beneath the cavernous ceilings of the station, past rows of high wooden pews. He felt as if he were deep inside a Roman bath. He found himself in a tunnel under the street and surfaced at the side door of the Château Laurier. So far he had not even seen Confusion Square. Choosing the first in a line-up of grey buses, he hopped aboard and crossed the Ottawa River for the third time that day, continuing into the country to the end of the line. Once again he was beside the river, this time twenty miles upstream, in Quebec. He'd been following the Ottawa but hadn't seen it because all those trees were in the way.

The factory where he'd found work that day was the one he worked in now, set off in a field at the crossroads that led to the tiny French village of St. Pierre, population four hundred. Four-thirty Saturday afternoon he noticed a sign, walked in, and got himself a job. Not in timber, but etching aluminum trays with fleurs-de-lis. Reason to move his family. Hope.

He thought of the small damp factory that would become his place of work, and of the large well-lit place he'd allowed himself to imagine. He became so depressed by his decision he continued along rue Principale to the one hotel, the St. Pierre, and asked for a beer. Again, he thought of his first look at the new place of work, all chimney and dark stone. He would carry the picture of it forever. What would Maura say, and where would he put her and the children? He drank three bottles of beer and turned to the man beside him at the bar, and with a clumsiness of hands and Ontario high-school French he asked when the next bus would leave the village. The man was English; his name was Duffy, and his wife had just run out on him. Duffy had lost out on life's grab for happiness but he had a real deal for Jock. He had a house to sell.

Jock had walked to the end of the village with Duffy and stood on the dirt road that overlooked river, rapids, pines. He'd allowed the view to enter him the way he had entered the view. He had not hesitated an instant before agreeing to take the bungalow off Duffy's hands.

Sunday noon, Trude fried cheese for her father. Oil burst through the Cheddar, oozing up from its own thick crust. She fried blood pudding in the same cast-iron pan. Sat at the kitchen table and ate the same meal. After Sunday school, it was the children's job to fend for themselves while Maura prepared the weekly roast and peeled the turnip and potatoes for supper.

Trude knew that Lyd would scoff at her cooking. Lyd kept telling her that blood pudding really *was* blood, congealed in animal intestine. As a matter of fact, it didn't look much like pudding to Trude; when she sliced it with a knife it was a pasty dark maroon. Their father was noncommittal while the blood-pudding argument was batted back and forth above his head. "That's enough," he finally said in his *tone-of-voice*, and the two girls shut up.

Aiming for his own bubble of peace, Jock began to chant, *"Wee, sleeket, cowran tim'rous beastie, O, what a panic's in thy breastie!"*

Trude glanced at her mother's back, at her mother's long dark hair swept into a roll, at the Sunday dress covered by an apron. She listened to her mother's silence and her father's poetry while she cleaned and scrubbed the cast-iron pan. It was her job to wash the Sunday midday dishes.

It was Trude's job, too, to write to Granny Tracks and let her know what the family was up to since Jock had moved them to Quebec. Granny Tracks was Maura's mother; her real name was Mary Meagher. She lived in Ontario in the same house she'd always lived in before Grandfather Meagher had died, but because the Darley trains ran close behind it, the children called her Granny Tracks.

Dear Granny Tracks,

I have my first paying job. Father hired me to roll cigarettes. He pays twenty-five cents a week. My fingers smell like tobacco.

Trude liked the job but it put her at her father's beck and call. Responsibility goes with a salaried position, he'd told her. It didn't seem to matter to him that she was next at bat or that he'd foiled a game of scrub. *One pah-tata two pah-tata three*

10

pah-tata four. She could hear the others dividing into teams, outside in the sun.

Trude created wondrous oversized cigarettes while seated at Jock's desk in the living room. She faced a wooden frame and a flat piece of red rolling rubber controlled at each end by a silver wheel. She tucked tobacco into the trough and inserted a delicately long strip of Vogue paper. She wet the edge with a cotton tip, tugged the wheels forward and *Voila!* Into the trench fell a fifteen-inch cigarette.

> Father says I have the touch. I can make a
> cigarette that's not scrawny with tobacco shreds
> sticking out of it, and not plump so it's bursting at
> the seams.

A half razor blade was stowed underneath, in a miniature compartment with a sliding cover. Trude sliced the giant cigarette into five reasonable ones and packed them into Father's silver case. When the case was full she snapped it shut. Job done.

Lyd's job, as eldest, was to sweep the house. She swept right through the long narrow bungalow one door to the other. She swept carpets until clouds of dust encompassed entire rooms. She put a record on the record player in the living room and sang "Jezebel" and then "Cold, Cold Heart." She twined her dark hair up to the top of her head and she kissed her own arm, pressing her lips to the softness of her skin. She whispered, "I love you," because she was practising and had every intention of being ready, when the first kisser came along.

After the sweeping was finished Lyd walked away from the

job. She walked away leaving heaps of dust and broom straw in doorways between rooms, exactly where she'd swept.

In winter, Eddie, the youngest, carried out the ashes and brought in the coal, but on hot days in summer it was his job to run up rue Principale between courses to buy a brick of ice cream for dessert. The others sat waiting, at the table. A long bar of sun lowered itself to the kitchen window and blazed into Trude's eyes. When Eddie came back with the ice cream, he was out of breath, his hair damp, his curls stuck to his forehead.

He set the brick beside the five stacked saucers in front of Maura, and he waited. The ice cream had to be eaten at one meal because the icebox in the summer kitchen could not keep it frozen.

Maura's job was to slice. She peeled back the cardboard until the sides flattened. She made four nicks across the surface, measuring for fairness. Each member of the family was served a band of pink, white and brown, the edges round with melting. Eddie, still panting from his run across the field, was permitted the scraping of the melted parts.

Jock's job, when he wasn't at the factory etching fleurs-de-lis onto aluminum trays, was to ensure that his children grew up and that they grew up well. He wanted them to know about poetry and imagination. He wanted them to know about life and danger, the sure connection between the two. When he first moved them to the village he took them to the ruins of the old hydro wall and showed them how the wall was crumbling outward over rapids. He told them never to lean against it, never, if they wanted to stay alive.

Later, binoculars around his neck, he stalked the river and

paced the bank. He inspected cloud formations above the waves and recited, *"For de win' she blow lak hurricane, Bimeby she blow some more."* He called his children down to shore in front of the house and taught them to memorize west by a sun that was sinking below the trees across the cove. If they learned west, they'd know east — sun rising over rapids — and south, a quarter turn to the right. "You can see a storm coming a mile away," he told them. "See those black clouds? In eight minutes, nine tops, they'll be hanging over the roof."

He rode the bus to Hull and bought a barometer at Kelly-Leduc. He installed it on the porch wall near the grinning sturgeon that had been mounted over the doorway and hung there with its bony scutes and hoselike snout. After the barometer, life was never the same. Jock taught the children high pressure, low pressure, how the arrow fluctuated before a storm and how it stilled in periods of stagnant heat. "Stand with your back to the wind," he told them. "Low pressure's on your left, high on your right." During summer storms they disappeared to the barn to play in the attic, but he came after them and shouted up from outside, "Barometer's changing, watch for the clearing! You should be able to see the whole thing from up there. Watch for the clearing. It's an amazing view."

Whether there was wind or hail or thunder, and though he wanted her to see the turbulence outside, Jock knew that he could not convince Maura to leave the kitchen. She refused to look through any window as she outwaited every storm.

On Fridays, Maura cooked liver and onions for Jock though she did not eat these herself. She knew that, back from the river, streets and streets of the Catholic neighbours she did not know were inside their houses eating tinned sardines. She knew, too, that in the summer they ate pickerel or bass from the river, sometimes even catfish, *barbotte*. Her own family caught and ate catfish, too. Jock cut off the heads on shore so she wouldn't have to look at their barbels and their rubbery snouts before she threw them, skinless, into the pan.

Maura had other jobs. Mondays, the wringer washer was pushed from the summer kitchen to the main kitchen, and two galvanized tubs for the rinse were set on kitchen chairs. The wringers swung back and forth over the tubs. When Lyd had been a toddler she'd climbed up and caught her hand between wringers. Whenever the story was told by Maura's mother in Darley, it always had the same ending: *Lydia, God-luv-'er, was lucky her entire arm wasn't mutilated.*

Trude had written to Granny Tracks to find out for herself:

> Is the story true? You were right there in the same town before we moved. Did you see Lyd's baby bones after they got whipped through the wringer? There's no scar. Mother says she slammed the quick release in the nick of time.

Trude wanted to check the facts because Lyd had begun to pull the story out of her past to flaunt it, even though she had no memory of the event. When Trude got sick and tired hearing about it she went down to the riverbank and ran back and forth across the stones to toughen up the soles of her feet. It was she who organized the bare foot race at the end of every summer.

On Tuesdays, Maura dipped the Monday-washed clothes into a bucket of starch and ironed while she listened to

"Pepper Young's Family." Wednesdays, the sewing machine was set up between dining room and kitchen because that was the only place the cord could be plugged in.

> Mother does everything in the kitchen. She drags the sewing machine in here even though it blocks the doorway and we have to squeeze past. She listens to the words of the radio songs and when she learns them, she sings them to us. She cuts up the material with pinking shears, and the leftover shapes get scattered around the linoleum. If we run out of toilet paper and someone uses a piece of pattern, Mother has to invent the missing shape. This makes her very mad. I am never going to be a housewife and I will never learn to sew. Mother made me sit in front of the Singer so she could teach me how to thread. I sat there for an hour before she let me go. I told her I'd never learn and I meant it. When she was a little child, did you force her to sew?

Maura listened as Lyd and Trude sang the French songs they'd learned the past year in their one-room school. Though Maura herself had managed not to learn a single word of French, she turned off her radio songs when the girls were singing. She caught the rhythm and hummed along beside her daughters and mouthed the strange and unfamiliar syllables into the vibrating air above their heads.

At the end of summer, the job of cleaning windows was assigned to Eddie and Trude, all windows, the entire house. Eddie was to use the ladder on the outside; Trude, the step-stool on the inside, starting with the room that was all windows, the porch.

"Work as a pair so you can get the streaks," Maura said. She handed each of them a bar of Bon-Ami, which they began to smooth down, rubbing at the whiteness of the bars with a wet cloth. Maura called the bars "Bawn-Ammy."

Trude and Eddie rubbed white all over the porch windows and circled out each other's faces and Trude printed S-H-I-T backwards across an inside pane and Eddie looked startled and then printed on the outside, P-I-S-, but not in mirror writing. Both words were shined off before Maura came to inspect for spots, but they kept it up all afternoon.

While they were thinking up obscenities to stretch all the way around the house, Lyd was told to polish the dining-room suite, Jock's smoker with its spool legs, and strips of wood that showed on the Queen Anne chairs. This was part of the furniture left behind by Duffy's runaway wife and after that by Duffy when he sold the house to Jock — lock, stock and barrel. Duffy's wife had run off with his best friend and Duffy had been too heartsick to carry so much as a tie-rack out the front door. After he'd clinched the deal, Jock had gone back to Darley to get Maura and the children and he'd listed off the contents, ending with the piano and the two Queen Anne chairs. Real ones. As if the chairs had been the deciding factor. Duffy had walked away from the treachery of woman and had taken a room in the village. Now, he was able to come right back into the house as Jock's friend and sit on his own chairs and switch on the pair of Tiffany lamps in the porch and look at himself in the long mirror that had held the image of his runaway wife. It didn't seem to bother him at all.

Lyd and Trude had been dragging an old argument forward since early morning. The argument was about whose turn it was to use the top drawer of their shared dresser, the one that had the extra space. Lyd thought she should have it because she was older and needed more things.

It hadn't been necessary to be in the same room until Trude had finally worked her way along the inside windows as far as the dining room. Lyd was already there, pouring a bubble of lemon oil onto the tabletop. She soaked the oil into the cloth and held the cloth away from her as the scent rose and hung before her face like a suffocating veil.

First she rubbed the wood, then she began to polish. Separate cloth. By the time she got to the rung of the first chair, she was bored. Trude was at the window trying to spell *diarrhea* backwards into the Bon-Ami-coated glass. She wasn't sure if the word had one *r* or two, and she didn't know about the *h*. Trude had won every spelling bee in her class but Mrs. Perry had never tested her limits with *diarrhea*.

D-I-A-R she printed. Lyd came up behind her and flicked the polishing cloth close to her ear. Trude turned and snapped the window cloth at Lyd. Their mother walked into the room.

"Cut it out," she said.

Maura had just washed her hair and was fastening a turban around her head. She held a hairbrush in her left hand.

"Lyd took a swipe at me first," said Trude. She added a *Y* to D-I-A-R and from outside Eddie pointed and shook the ladder, laughing.

"They're writing dirty words on the windows," Lyd said. "They're so juvenile." She flicked her cloth at Trude again, catching her on the shoulder.

"D-I-A-R-Y," Trude spelled. "What's dirty about that? Dear Dirty Diary."

"Cut it out," said Maura. "I've already told you once."

Trude flicked her cloth back at Lyd when she believed her mother was leaving the room. Maura's body turned and the hairbrush left her open palm. It flew across the room and struck the wall between chair and window, between Lyd and Trude. The three of them heard the *crack* as the brush broke in two, missing the girls by inches.

Maura returned to pick up the pieces and walked out of the room. She did not apologize and she did not excuse herself in any way.

Trude watched her mother's back tighten as she left the room. Because the broken pieces were gone, Trude was not certain, now, that Maura had thrown the brush.

Lyd's face had whitened but there were red patches on her cheeks. She looked at Trude and pushed a chair in front of the mark on the wall. "Damn you and damn Mother, both," said Lyd, under her breath. "*I'm* staying on this side of the room and *you* stay on that one."

Trude glanced again towards the empty doorway, and felt a quickening in her chest. She climbed down from the stepstool and stood there, not knowing what to do. She set her cloth on the floor and waited, and as there was no other noise in the house, she went to find the dictionary so she could learn to spell the word *diarrhea*.

———————————

When Eddie had finished his part of the job, he walked to the Pines, between cove and rapids. He lay on his belly at the edge of the cliff and stared at the water. He clung to the roots of some tangled bushes, peered over and, without thinking, began to climb down. The roots were above his head as he tested with one foot, for a ledge. He let go when he felt something solid, crouched as he dropped, his back to the river, and landed facing a small cave. To his surprise he could turn his body around and fit inside.

The cave was lined with layers of horizontal rock. At first, Eddie sat with his chin on his knees and wondered about the place. His sisters would want to know. But if he were to tell them, it wouldn't belong to him.

He thought of his mother's face as he'd watched her through the window from the ladder, outside. He did not know what was wrong but he'd seen her throw the brush at Lyd and Trude. He broke off pieces of rock and threw them into fast water below.

If his father found out about the cave he would say, *Stay away. The cave will crumble.* Jock was always threatening about the wall, too, the wall that tilted over rapids. Eddie looked towards the ruins, far to his left, and tried to imagine the wall crumpling like caved-in knees. So far, the wall had not begun to fall.

Swallows had gathered and now swooped and glided above the river. Eddie broke off a large piece of rock and tossed it hard into their midst. Though he did not intend to hit a bird, though he did not hear the thunk, he felt it, as a swallow disappeared. Its wings folded as it entered the blue-black swirl of river. Eddie's breath stopped. He had not meant to kill a bird. He should not even be in the cave. He did not move for a long time, frozen by the fear that if he moved, he, too, would thud into dark water.

Dear Granny Tracks,

We will soon be back in school. We went to the Ottawa Ex and saw Elsie the Borden Cow and got a bag of free samples from the Pure Food Building. Lyd won a lamp in bingo and had to carry it all the way home on the bus.

Father fired me from my cigarette-rolling job. He was in the St. Pierre Hotel all ready to clinch a deal on a secondhand Hoover. He offered cigarettes to the men around him and he held up the flame but the cigarettes fell apart when the men sucked in. I think I put too much water on the sticky edge. Father came home roaring mad but I don't care. The men laughed hard but Father got the Hoover. He says we're bloody lucky he doesn't have to kick Lyd's dust piles around the house any more. When he came back he grabbed his binoculars and went down to the river to look at the view but I don't know what he could see, it was so dark.

I found out that Mrs. Perry is going to be my teacher again. She thinks the St. Lawrence River runs downhill. I keep showing her on the map that it runs up. We still have to take the bus out of the village with all the other Protestants, to our one-room school called "Stone." Geoffrey Babble will have a fit the first week of September. The last day of school in June, he was sitting in front of me and banged his head on my desk when he fell over.

Love, Trude

P.S. Today the river is the colour of dark green bottles, with raging rippling current. Mrs. Perry likes scenery and adjectives so I am getting some ready. There was a portage near our place, she said, because of the rapids. The Indians carried their canoes on their heads, or like that.

P.P.S. I won the bare foot race again this year.

Sunday morning, Jock was savouring the warmth of his bed, drifting in and out of sleep. There was a beat in his head, something endless and pulsing. He tried to recover it as he would a lost dream.

He thought of the factory. He'd etched so many fleurs-de-lis onto aluminum, he'd lost count. He felt the instrument in his hand, smelled the harshness of acid, wondered irrationally how many fleurs-de-lis it would take to feed his children until they grew up. He pushed this from his mind and flexed his hands under the sheet.

From factory rooms of dank dark stone he'd disseminated the French lily across the living breadth of Canada. There were some who thought the lily resembled the top of a battleaxe but he, Jock, held in his mind the picture of its three-fold beauty and its tight encircling ring. In his own home he was running out of space to stack the culls the factory could not sell. Maura had never complained. The workers had been asked to cart the seconds away, and Jock had carted away his share. From the stacks, only he could withdraw a tray and locate the imperfection that prevented it from being sent out, a shining harbinger to the territories and provinces. He saw each failed tray as a kind of rare stamp. He'd been bestowing trays on friends and relatives for Christmas, birthdays and anniversaries but, despite this, in all the corners of the house there was a rising tide of fleurs-de-lis.

Jock drifted again and woke as if someone had pinned his arms to his sides. The beat came back to his head. He was surrounded by shifting shadows of rock. Again he thought of the factory, saw the roar of furnace, heard the pounding of machine that flattened the trays before they glided towards him on the ever-moving belt.

He thought of Maura, and felt the picture of silence. He realized that he'd never known what Maura thought of the job he'd found after all that searching; what she thought of the hiring of the truck to transport their few belongings; of moving her and the children, on the train, away from Darley, Ontario, and into Quebec. It was what he'd had to do. A man had to feed his family. He'd lifted the atlas down from the shelf and had felt the silence of his wife. It was as if he'd been pulling her body away as his thumb traced its way down and back up the splendid solid curve of the grey and shadowy Shield.

Jock closed his eyes, tugged at the blanket, wrapped it tightly around him. The beat was still there, in his head.

Cannon to right of them, he thought. *Cannon to left of them.* And then, without effort, his head recited:

> Cannon in front of them
>   Volleyed and thundered;
> Stormed at with shot and shell,
> Boldly they rode and well,
> Into the jaws of Death,
> Into the mouth of Hell
>   Rode the six hundred.

Maura had been having dreams about the Queen Anne chairs. The ones left behind by Duffy's runaway wife. Maura had begun to hate the Queen Anne chairs. It was not the chairs so much as what they stood for. Maura, surrounded by someone else's furniture, wanted something of her own, not second-hand or antique or left behind by someone's runaway wife.

She'd often thought about the runaway wife. What it would take to walk through summer kitchen and kitchen, dining room, living room and porch, out the front door and down the steps. *Never look back,* Maura said to herself while she scrubbed stains out of collars, while she baked macaroni and cheese and sponged feverish torsos and counted out money for Paris-Patty sandwiches the children carried to school. *Never look back.* She thought of Lot's wife but Lot's wife had turned. Duffy's runaway wife had kept on going. Maura imagined this predecessor of her own kitchen and bedroom wearing red the day she left. It never occurred to her that Duffy's wife might have sneaked out the back door.

Maura walked the length of the house, from summer kitchen to glassed-in porch. Each room held its own silence as she passed. She stifled a whiff of anger as her fingertips brushed the backs of the Queen Anne chairs. She stood at the front screen and listened to the roar of rapids. She recognized the sound of sorrow.

Jock was at the tray factory; the children, eight miles away, in their one-room school. A breeze was puffing in off the river and the leaves of the tallest poplar were spinning. The maples across the cove flared in crimson patches. Maura loved the fall so much she could hardly bear it, each year, when the season began. She knew the day of its beginning, always in late August when the air changed. She could smell the fall the moment it arrived, the promise of a long season of wondrous colour and sad warmth. She wanted to run in the fall, run through the fields and towards the trees and along the river. *Run, Maura, Run,* she said, standing at the screen. She breathed fall-tipped air deep into her lungs.

She walked back through the house and started in the kitchen. She pushed the warped and wooden table to the back door, bumped it around the side of the house and dragged it down to the river. She returned for the kitchen chairs, the pair of Tiffany lamps from the porch and the tea wagon she never used except to park the plaster lamp encircled by Spanish dancers that Lyd had won in bingo at the Ottawa Ex. Maura rolled the tea wagon over the rocks. Every time she took out a piece of furniture, she exposed another stack of Jock's imperfect trays. The last two items she dragged out were the Queen Anne chairs.

Next, she went to the barn and picked up the long-handled axe. Collected paper from the top of the woodbin and stuffed three wooden matches into her pocket. She returned to the river, pushed furniture and lamps close together, and chopped randomly and with joy. She built her fire, wedged paper between splinters, threw in a match and sat a few feet back on layered shale. She thought of nothing but the flames. Listened to the crackling of the dismembered armrests of the Queen Anne chairs. Watched with light-headedness as they burned.

When there was nothing left but smouldering ashes and hot nails and melted parts, Maura returned to her empty kitchen. Sat on the floor and opened the Eaton's catalogue. Reached for the phone and dialled the number. Took a deep breath and heard her own voice order a brand-new shining seven-piece chrome suite.

Dear Granny Tracks,

This week Mother chopped some of the furniture while we were at school. I am not supposed to put this in the letter. She dragged the furniture down to the river and made a bonfire. Father was very mad but Mother was mad, too. Eaton's truck came and now we have a new table-and-chair set in the kitchen.

I have a best friend, now. Her name is Mimi. She is Catholic so she gets to stay in the village to go to the French school and the Catholic church. Everyone in Mimi's family is short. Mimi's feet are only size four. Mother says Lyd's feet grow longer every time the clock ticks.

Mimi's grand-mère lives with her family. Grand-mère's bones are so tiny Mimi can wrap two fingers around her wrists. Grand-mère laughs when I tell her *Little Red Riding Hood* in French.

"*Je m'appelle le Petit-Chaperon rouge. Je vais chez ma grand-mère.*" Red Riding Hood's *grand-mère* does not get eaten in French, don't worry. Ha Ha.

Lyd still dares me to do things because she knows I will take any dare except to dive headfirst into the river. Mother says if I keep it up, I won't live long enough for it to matter. Mother doesn't know, but Lyd double-dared me to stick two fingers into the pantry light socket. The electricity fired me against the pantry wall. Eddie and Lyd were both scared but they didn't tell.

Mother says that because I am her child-between it is my job to see both ways, forward and back. When I grow up, she says, I am the one who will be doomed to tell the family stories.

Love, Trude.

TRUDE

NEW YEAR, 1953

I was excited about the arrival of Granny Tracks, who came to visit the third week of December. Our entire family rode the bus to Hull and then the streetcar across the bridge and past the Chaudière Falls, to meet her at Ottawa's Union Station. This took an hour and a half each way. When she stepped through the iron gate, I was surprised to see our cousin Georgie — known to us as Georgie-Porgie — right behind her. He was the same age as Lyd; we'd coloured Shredded Wheat cards together in the backyard of our old place when we'd lived in Darley. We seldom saw him except when we returned to Ontario in the summer; he'd shot up half a foot and was now taller than Lyd.

The air was cold and clear when we got back to St. Pierre; our family had been the only travellers on the bus and, except for Mother, who refused to abandon Granny, we'd placed ourselves all around the bus in different corner seats, as if we were strangers. We walked across the field to our road, chemin Brébeuf, and Granny Tracks stood on our front step, her back to the river, to let Father know that she'd been dropped into the Quebec wilderness. It was still early evening. Mother and Granny said they were going in to whip up a meal, but Father kept the rest of us outside.

Lyd was appalled.

"Oh, great. Weekly winter walk," she said. "What's Georgie-Porgie going to say about this?"

Georgie had to set his suitcase inside the cold porch and join, whether he wanted to or not. Father initiated the walks in November of each year at the first sign of snow. No one was excused unless bedridden or struck down by fever. Cold weather was meant to keep us healthy.

Round and round the village streets, we tried to keep pace in the dark. Our boots crunched on snow while Father's voice kept up its relentless quiz. He didn't ask questions, he said them.

"Nine plus eight! Ten plus eleven! Multiply by two and carry one! Simplify, do it in your head, no fingers, no tapping fingers!" He knew Lyd hated math.

He tried to trick us, catch us off guard. "What colour was Napoleon's white horse. Which weighs more, a pound of coal or a pound of feathers."

The problems became more difficult. "Spell *parliament*, *cinnamon*, *enigma*! What does *perpetual* mean! *Instigate*! *Investigate*!"

He circled back to mental arithmetic, his favourite, setting up a competition as he strode. "First one who knows the answer — shout it out! Twelve times eleven, divide by six, times seven, add nine!"

All the while, we ran along beside him. And our answers, shouted back, held an icy desperate ring.

Lyd and I were humiliated having to face Georgie-Porgie in the porch light. I was terrified that Father would remove his scarf and gloves only to make a sudden charge into the living room, spouting poetry. Once started, his poetry was unstoppable. Georgie, forced to drag himself around the village, surprised us by blurting out, as soon as we took him to Eddie's room to show him his top bunk, that *his* father had chased his mother around the house with a butcher knife. They'd sent Georgie to us while they were sorting things out. His father, Uncle Weylin, was Granny Tracks's only son. The story was that Weylin had married a temperamental Irishwoman, Aunt Arra, who'd once kept house in northern England for a duke. Granny Tracks was glad her son had married Irish but thought her daughter-in-law affected. Maybe, we told Georgie, maybe your father isn't Weylin, but the duke. We were thinking of money. After all, Georgie had an English name.

We knew we couldn't be mean to him after he blurted out the stuff about his parents; what irritated us was that he reeked of the sufferer. We were suspicious, too, because he did not seem to think our family unreasonable. He said he liked Father but we threatened to pound him when he admitted that he was glad he'd joined us in our weekly winter walk.

"Jesus Cripes," Lyd said, "he's desperate for a father."

We were called for supper and Father squeezed in a chair for Georgie-Porgie between Eddie and me. Mother and Granny had served up bowls of thick homemade soup and set a plate of buttered bread, cut into ladyfingers, at each end of the table. We used our best manners and passed around a tray of soda biscuits and *Chateau* cheese, my favourite kind, flecked with pimento. I watched as Georgie pressed two soda biscuits between his palms and crumbled them into his soup, something we never did. I could see, too, that he had an eye on the Christmas baking that Mother had laid out on the shelf of the flour cupboard. I thought about Georgie being desperate for a father and I turned and stared at our own father, who was seated, unsuspecting, at the head of the table.

After the dishes were done we cleared the table and sat back down around it. Lyd was working on her Royal scrapbook. Her Scottish penpal had just sent her a newspaper copy of the family photo on this year's Royal Christmas card. Lyd was the only one in our entire school who had it. She'd found her penpal's name on the back page of one of Eddie's *Scrooge* comics; they wrote to each other all the time. The caption under the photo explained that the Queen and her family were standing on the steps of historic Balmoral Castle. I looked at Princess Anne and could see that she was gritting her teeth, probably because she was forced to stand still. Her hands were clenched into fat little fists. Charles looked pleased and patient beside his father, who was wearing a kilt. Elizabeth was wearing a skirt filled with pleats. She was not going to be crowned until next June but, at school, Mrs. Perry had already made us substitute the word *Queen* in "God save our gracious. . . ." Both Mrs. Perry and the Queen, I could tell from the photo, wore the same kind of laced-up high-platformed shoes.

Georgie was slumped at one end of the table, fatigued and sad-looking. Except for Granny Tracks and Lyd, the others had left the room.

I started working on Granny to tell us about Grandfather

Meagher, dead before I was born. Before any grandchild, for that matter. There were so few photographs on either side — Meaghers and Kings — Lyd said the two families must have dirt to hide. One tintype of Grandfather Meagher did exist but this was back in Ontario, in Granny's Darley home. It was kept in a cigar box in her rolltop desk and we seldom got to see it. The tintype was bent lengthwise through the middle and Grandfather Meagher's sepia face was trapped in this permanent concave fault. Even so, I was certain from the erectness of his posture that if he were alive, we would not be calling him Grampa Tracks.

I had often thought of him in school when practising the sixteen *être* verbs, glancing up at the row of cardboard charts above the blackboards. My tongue passed over *mourir*. Mrs. Perry had shrieked, "You can't use the past tense of *mourir* with *je!*" Because it was forbidden, I murmured as I conjugated — *Je suis mort, tu es mort, il est mort* — thinking of Grandfather Meagher. I imagined him whispering the past tense in the first person to spite Mrs. Perry, at the split second of his last breath.

"Tell us, Granny. What did he look like? What colour was his hair? Did he shout?" All the men I knew shouted. Father. Duffy. Uncle Weylin. Grampa King. Father's friends. They shouted every time they met one another: *How are ya', you old son of a gun? How the hell are you?*

Granny Tracks seemed annoyed for a moment; she'd been through this line of questioning before. She looked at a pad of foolscap lying on the kitchen cabinet behind me and reached out a hand.

"Give me a piece of paper," she said. "A ruler, a good one with a steel edge. And a pencil."

Lyd looked up from her scrapbook.

33

"I can see his face so clearly," said Granny, as if she'd dropped into a trance.

Georgie perked up.

She began to line the paper, cross-hatching, covering the sheet with squares, shading here and there.

"I can see his face so clearly," she said. Louder, this time. She was filling in the squares to shape a head.

Father walked into the kitchen and looked over her shoulder. He cackled. "Paint by number?"

Granny Tracks ignored him. Thinking he might have hurt her feelings, I said, "She's drawing Grandfather Meagher."

Father shot through to the living room. "Now I've seen everything," I heard him say to Mother. "She's drawing a graph of your father's face."

Granny Tracks moaned. "Your grandfather Meagher scratched a cross in the dirt with the toe of his boot, the day before he died."

"*Il est mort*," I whispered.

When the drawing was done, two off-balance eyes glowered out of the squares. The hair was black and thick and high. There was no room for ears, as his cheeks touched both edges of the page. His nose was bumpy and unrealistic. Granny didn't know about perspective. The mouth, though, could have been the mouth of a real person. This face had no age that I could tell.

Granny Tracks was not unpleased. She held up the paper and laughed. "First thing I've drawn in my entire life," she said. Lyd and I laughed, too, thinking this a great joke. I wondered what Mother would say if I showed her.

"Sign it, Granny," I said. She did and I took it to my room and looked at it again, and then I flattened it into my bottom drawer.

Georgie turned on us. He went past our bedroom, later, and stuck his head through the doorway and said, "Your whole family is nutso."

"They're your family, too, Puddin' and pie," Lyd said.

"He's probably suffering from exhaustion," I said, thinking of the weekly winter walk.

A long closet, it was really a dark tunnel, crossed the width of the house and joined the living room to my bedroom. Not only mine; I shared the double bed with Lyd. The chimney was at our end of the tunnel, and shelves and cupboards had been built to the ceiling at the living-room end. The rest of the space was used for out-of-season coats and for storing bedding. Just past the chimney there were three plastic garment bags, each with a collapsible cardboard bottom. Right after Christmas, the garment bags were unzipped, the contents laid out on Mother's bed.

Here were the pastel dresses Mother created; here were strapless taffeta gowns, an abundance of crinolined skirts, strapless bras, ribboned evening bags and dyed satin shoes. Here Mother had fashioned a world from *Vogue*. A world unconnected to St. Pierre or Darley or to any world that I could call up. Five women who sewed had found one another in the village and formed a club. Mother was the sixth; her induction had balanced the group, half-English, half-French. One of the women was Duffy's new girlfriend, Rebecque, whom Lyd and I adored. She said things to us like, "Always dab your perfume where there's a pulse. *Ici! Ici!*" Jabbing one finger at the veins of her wrist, her temple, the side of her slender neck.

Mother's latest creation, made during the fall, was a mauve strapless dress with net overlay and a stole of the same colour rising up behind her shoulders like stiff pale flames. Twice a year, New Year's Eve and early summer, the women of the club mustered their men and held a party at one of the homes, so far not ours.

This year, the New Year's Eve party was at the home of Mona and Roy. Mona of the bound feet. Though she never talked about her childhood, the story was that forty-six years earlier, Mona had been born into a wealthy family on the Mongolian border. Her nurse had bound her baby feet until Mona had been almost crippled. By the time Mona immigrated to Canada, she was walking with tiny little steps. Lyd, whose feet were already growing alarmingly long, gawked at Mona's feet every chance she could get.

Lyd and I had heard the rest of the story while eavesdropping on Mother and Rebecque. Mona's parents had lost their fortune but Mona had had a stroke of luck when she was eighteen. While working as a waitress in a bistro in Montreal, she'd been wiping a tabletop and looked down into the eyes of Roy, who was visiting the city for a day. Instant love, we were told. It was as if they'd been lovers in some other, previous life. They married and moved to the village of St. Pierre. They were older than the other couples in the club and had no children; the barren Mona was not lucky at *everything*, Rebecque told our mother.

I watched as Mother studied herself in the bedroom and bathroom mirrors. Her black hair had been pulled back and pinned, and in those moments I believed that generations of women in our family had somehow betrayed the Irish by bestowing on their female progeny traces of Spanish blood. A stubby white jar of deodorant, a wide powder puff I had given her for Christmas, a touch of rouge over each cheekbone — Mother managed these as casually as if she stepped into formal dress two or three times a week. Lyd stood close by so that she would be the one to be asked to zip Mother's dress from behind. Mother hummed to herself as she chose rhinestone earrings and a choker that sparkled like diamonds, and then Lyd and I sat on her bed, our cheeks as flushed as hers as she arranged her stole, crimping it between her fingers to round the folds. She dabbed lavender perfume behind her ears and raised her chin to the mirror to put on her lipstick, last of all. Lyd and I preceded her out the bedroom door, as if we were presenting her to the rest of the family.

The transformation silenced Father. He was never comfortable when he was dressed up and he fidgeted, now, while Eddie circled him and brushed his jacket.

We stood back, away from them, when the one and only village taxi arrived, as if being close might muss them up in some base family way. Granny Tracks was being dragged along with them and she stood, solemn and celebratory, in her plain black dress and strand of pearls. She travelled with these everywhere, she said, in case of invitation.

The house was suddenly emptied of glamour. Left alone, and feeling plain, we turned out the lights and sat on the chesterfield, waiting for midnight.

Each of us had a quart bottle of soft drink stuck between our knees and we swigged at these in controlled sips so there'd be something left to toast in the New Year. Mine was grapefruit and lime. After Christmas, Father had given us money to go up rue Principale to Le Loup's to choose. We'd packed the tall bottles and some extra ginger ale into a box and rattled it back on our wooden sleigh.

Georgie had been uncomplaining the past few days, knowing he needed us to survive. For one thing, after the Christmas bones had been picked, we'd carried him through four nights of turkey soup. The house rule was that you couldn't leave the table until you'd finished what had been put before you.

"Have a bowl of swamp soup," we said cheerily, knowing it made him gag.

But we helped Georgie by swapping bowls, a continuous round of trickery that enabled him to leave the table.

He'd remained silent when Father had marched us around the village again, shouting out, "*Half a league, half a league, Half a league onward.*" And he needed us outside, too — needed our French words when we took him to the store, needed our familiarity with every inch of riverbank and every fingergrip in the old hydro wall that leaned over the rapids. He needed us at the rink we'd cleared on the river in front of the house, where we practised teapot and swan, and he needed us to guide him over thin ice on the swamp behind the barn.

What Georgie had that we did *not* know was an unstoppable repertoire of horror stories and these he began to unleash as we sat in the dark, knees drawn up, petrified, sliding towards 1953. After two hours of bloody headless creatures he was droning in measured voice about ghosts that left no footprints, ghosts that drifted over fast waters and through the walls of lonely country homes. Ghosts that could be near at that very moment, the ebb of the old year. It was almost midnight and no one, not even Georgie, dared to put a foot on the floor. Eddie had pulled his sweater up over his head and refused to budge. After all the swigging at our bottles every one of us had to pee and it was Lyd, finally, who broke the spell. She crawled along the back of the chesterfield and stretched to reach the lamp switch. Georgie looked like pathetic Georgie again, in the light. But I could still hear his scaring voice in my ears.

We pretended we hadn't been scared.

We tuned the floor-model radio in the living room to an Ottawa station across the river that took requests, and decided to phone in a dedication. Our mother loved radio, our mother loved song. I was at the phone end of the chair and kept a finger in the dial but couldn't get through. I tried Father's trick. If you dialled all the numbers but one, you'd block out the hundreds of other desperadoes. After a long pause, I dialled the last number. A man's voice shouted. I shouted back.

"Play 'Lady of Spain' ... for our mother ... from Lyd Trude Eddie Georgie ... her children ... with love!" I didn't want to get into complications of Georgie being a cousin; there was too much noise in the station background. I could see that Georgie was pleased.

"Does 'our mother' have a name?" the man said sarcastically.

I hung up. We laughed ourselves silly we were so excited, and we turned up the volume. We phoned Mother at Mona's and the noise there was worse than it had been at the station. It took some time before Mother came to the phone. We told her we had a surprise for her, that she had to listen to the radio. It didn't occur to us that if Mother had to listen, the whole party had to listen. Right at twelve o'clock.

It was the first day of the year and Father came home from the party alone and in a cast. He'd made a bet with Roy, Mona's husband, that there was black ice on the stones below their front steps. At two in the morning he'd gone outside in his stocking feet and slid across the ice, a glass of whisky held high in his right hand. He dropped the glass and broke his ankle, and after the men dragged him up the steps, Roy phoned for the taxi. Duffy accompanied Father across the Champlain Bridge to hospital. Mona drove Mother and Granny home, pressing the pedals of Roy's big car with her tiny feet. We still hadn't gone to bed, though we were all asleep on the chesterfield. Mother's eyes were red and she curtly told us to get into our beds.

Father had to wait three hours in X-ray and Emergency until one of the doctors had time to take him to the Plaster Room to do the cast. Even though the cast was wet, Duffy was the first to sign: *Shame on you, you old screw.* All New Year's Day Father sat in his armchair in the living room, his leg elevated on the hassock. He'd had no sleep.

More interesting to me was Canada's first New Year's baby, born at the same Ottawa hospital in which Father and Duffy had sat waiting most of the night, three floors below. They'd heard the news, Father said. It was like a zoo in there. Everyone except the mortally wounded had been celebrating.

The last paper of the year had run a front-page spread of Father Time slipping past one side of the clockface, the Peace Tower clock of Parliament Hill. A cheery-looking toddler in diapers was emerging from the other side, the one o'clock side. I knew better but imagined this baby to be the newborn reported on the radio. There'd been an argument, the broadcast said, between Ottawa and Moose Jaw, over which baby took its first breath in the fraction of a second after midnight. Ottawa had been declared winner. Its baby girl would receive free diapers, a pink carriage and a year's supply of baby food.

From across the icy river, from the western fringes of Quebec, we felt that our baby had won.

Granny Tracks and Mother were giving Father the cold shoulder, so the rest of us felt that we had to, as well. We did not speak to him directly or give any sign that we approved of his behaviour. This was not easy because a steady stream of visitors came through the door, all afternoon, paying homage, signing Father's cast.

Mother had heard "Lady of Spain" at Mona's but it hadn't been played until ten past one in the morning. Loyal to her children she'd sat with one ear to Mona's kitchen radio in the noisiest room of the party, the bar.

We were happy about our fame and bragged about it to everyone who visited: our names, even Georgie's, had been broadcast for the world to hear throughout Ottawa and West Quebec.

At dinner that night, Father stood at the end of the dining-room table, carving our second turkey in a week. Still rebuffed by the women, he dangled the bird's rear in the air and said loudly, "Who wants the pope's nose?"

Granny Tracks, remembering her mixed Protestant-Catholic beginnings, did not acknowledge the insult. She gathered herself together and muttered in monotone to anyone who would hear, "One January first I nearly killed your grandfather Meagher. I fed him roast pork and he almost died. He chewed the meat too close to the bone and sucked the marrow. He threw up for two days and two nights and the cries that came from the sickroom drowned the noise of the trains."

We stared at our plates.

I thought of Grampa's ageless, earless face flattened into

my bottom drawer, his graphed mouth coughing up chunks of roast pork.

Georgie looked as if he might throw up. He also knew he'd be facing four more nights of turkey soup. At least he'd escaped the weekly winter walk. But that was not to be. Between turkey and plum pudding, Father banged his cast against the table leg and said to Lyd and Eddie, Georgie and me, "Get up, we're going outside. Never mind your coats."

We preceded Father out the front door, which he left open wide behind him. The rapids snuffed all other sound. So accustomed were we to the roar, we only heard it when there was a visitor, opening our ears in politeness. In the moonlight, mist rose as if its shifting shroud concealed not a river but a vast and unbroken moor. Ice stretched out from the cove but every one of us knew that the current was black and swift beneath.

"Out with the old!" Father broke all sound, shouting in ceremonial voice. He turned the corner of the house. He led our procession not the length of the shovelled path but past the raspberry bushes on the other, snowy side, the side that was never used in winter. As we followed, we tried to fit our feet into knee-deep holes his cast had punched through the snow.

We rushed the storm door at the back of the house, trying to escape his town-crier behaviour.

"In with the new!" he shouted.

Georgie dragged himself in after us. *His* father might have chased his mother with a butcher knife but his father was not like ours.

Cold air had swept through every room of the house. Mother had rushed from the table to close the front door behind us on our way out but she was too late; the heat had escaped. She sat back down and stared stonily ahead.

From the dining room Granny Tracks looked from one to another as we swept snow from our shoes with the broom, as we hopped from one foot to the other in the kitchen, and blew on our hands. She grabbed the cardigan that hung from the back of her chair and draped it tightly around her.

"Crazyman," she said. She turned her back on us. "My daughter married a crazyman."

Hearing this, Georgie looked satisfied.

In that instant, I wished to be distanced from my father. If I could have, I'd have exchanged my entire set of relatives, Granny Tracks and Georgie included, for some other reasonable, normal family.

After Granny and Georgie had returned to Darley on the train and after we'd gone back to school, I saw a photograph taken the night of Mona's New Year's party. Black and white, it was the club of six with their husbands and Duffy. Granny Tracks was missing because she was behind the camera.

I studied the twelve faces. Even though the photo was not in colour I could see the mauve of Mother's taffeta and I could detect the wayward Spanish blood. I could smell the lavender perfume and the powder she'd patted over her cheeks to take away the shine. But her face seemed small, somehow. I worried when I thought about the photo, later.

She had been leaning forward with some of the other women. The men were standing at the sides and behind and some of them looked roaring drunk. Most of them wore conical hats perched on their heads, an elastic under the chin. The women in their *Vogue* creations looked perky, strained, as if they'd turned up at the wrong party and were making the best of it. Mona had opted for a long dress, concealing her little feet. Mother was holding her lips together as if she were waiting for someone who had decided at the last minute not to come. Duffy held an enamel pee-pot, upside down, over my father's head.

MIRACLES

1953

On the last day of June, Mimi's sister Pierrette got up in the night to use the pee-pot and looked out the upstairs window. A mile and a half across the river, she could see Ottawa lights twinkling like stars along the Richmond Road. There was a high mist at the end of the rapids below.

She looked down then and saw a woman, upright between waves. The woman, facing her, did not tilt one way or another. She raised her left hand and moved it back and forth as if to say, *Non! Non!*

Bee-Bee, the new stepfather, had just moved into the house and Pierrette took the sign to mean disapproval. Pierrette and Mimi's own father had died in a logging accident only a year before. Pierrette had refused to attend her mother's wedding.

Mimi had told me all of this, but I learned about the

woman in the rapids only on Saturday morning when I arrived to find everyone sitting around the breakfast table in their robes and pyjamas. Grand-mère, in the kitchen rocker, was pitching back and forth as if she were sailing a high sea. She was glad to see me.

I never knew who belonged to whom, so many people lived in that house. Outside staircases threaded up and down the building but there were few territorial divisions inside. Two men lived there — Bee-Bee and Mimi's uncle, Henri — but mostly there were women: sisters; and aunts old and young. "*Mes tantes*," Mimi called them. I thought of them as the aunts of the little bones.

Not one woman in Mimi's family had ever grown taller than the height of a twelve-year-old. Pierrette, the eldest of Mimi's sisters and the last to be married except for Mimi, was also the most petite. Pierrette had a fiancé, Ferdinand, a six-foot bulk of a man who'd just opened a small grocery store in the village. He planned to move Pierrette away from the big house and the new stepfather, and into two rooms above the store — with plumbing.

Bee-Bee, who claimed to know only four words of French, three of them bad, was grilling Pierrette in English, trying to verify facts.

"What was the woman wearing?" he said. "What colour were her clothes?"

"There was no colour," said Pierrette coolly. "Everything was misty."

"And she was standing in the middle of the rapids."

"Floating upright," she said. "More like that."

"Was she on the Quebec side?"

"Definitely."

Mimi's mother was trying to keep the peace between Bee-Bee and her daughter. The aunts wrung their hands. *"Un miracle,"* they murmured, and they looked away from one another.

I ran home through the Pines and up the back steps. Mother was getting ready to take the eleven o'clock bus to Hull to order groceries from the A&P. I told her and Father about the miracle but they ignored that part. Mother had just pulled on her white gloves and was stepping into her spectator pumps at the kitchen door. She paused to look down. Her toes and heels looked as if they'd been dipped into a vat of old chocolate.

"All those people in the one house," she said. "And no indoor plumbing. I couldn't do it. A pee-pot," she said.

"It's a miracle *anyone* has a pot to pee in after this many years of Duplessis," Father said.

I saw that neither of them could be expected to understand. After Mother crossed the field, I went to my room and lifted my Bible cards from the bottom drawer. Every week after Sunday school in Hull, I brought a new card home and placed it next to the graphed and shaded drawing of dead Grandfather Meagher — signed by his widow, Granny Tracks. First I looked at Granny's drawing. I stared at the glowering brows and studied the face. I erased the eyebrows and drew in thinner kinder ones and placed the picture back in the bottom drawer. Then I shuffled the Bible cards and arranged them clock-shape on my bedspread. Beneath a picture of the crumbling city of Jericho, a caption read: *The people shouted with a great shout, that the wall fell down flat.* I also owned, *Christ sendeth out the twelve; Jairus' daughter raised to life; The fish vomiteth out Jonah upon the dry land.*

My favourite was *Christ feedeth the five thousand.* I held it in my palm, wishing I'd been there. Jesus stood at the bottom of a crowded hill and behind Him was the shoving multitude that followed Him everywhere. Andrew, Simon Peter's brother, was gesturing towards *the lad* who was lucky enough to be holding five barley loaves and two fishes. Andrew was watching Jesus' face to see what He would do. It was clear that Andrew was hoping for a miracle.

There were many night trips to the pee-pot now, a steady parade of aunts taking turns and then pausing at the window on tiptoe to peer down at the waves. Grand-mère said she was glad she had a room downstairs on the far side of the house where she didn't have to worry, at her age, about miracles and the river.

Bee-Bee made fun of the aunts. He came into the kitchen with a bucket of water and lifted the lid of the reservoir that took up the whole side of the big stove.

"Anybody for a miracle? Watch," he said. "Empty!" He poured. "Full! It would be a miracle," he said, "if anybody besides me ever carried a full pail into this house."

He reached into the reservoir and flicked a sprinkling of water at Mimi and me. He ducked out the door and Mimi's mother shouted after him, "You know Henri can't lug the buckets because of his leg in the war!" She turned to us. "Don't play with water in the house," she said, but we'd already chased out after him with a glass of water.

Bee-Bee played with us like that. If we were finishing a game of hide-and-seek at dusk, and sneaking up to a corner of the house to see if home-free was safe, Bee-Bee would charge around the corner and shout, terrifying us as we screamed and ran. Because there was a big rain barrel filled with water at the back stoop, there seemed to be water fights, too, continuously, during the hot evenings of summer. The rainwater was collected by the aunts, who used it as rinse water to make their hair silky. If we were in a dry spell, they had to add vinegar to the rinse water, instead.

Despite the lugging of every drop of water, even the aunts and the visiting sisters and their children sometimes joined in at the peak of the *water wars*, as Mimi and I called them. Someone would always take someone else by surprise and douse them with a full bucket of water. I had never known adults to play like that, everyone worked up to a high pitch, hurling threats, gasping and laughing and running back inside to sit around the kitchen table, and then jumping up and taking off again. There was always one last person soaked to the skin, seeking revenge, and that last person would never give up. When it was Bee-Bee, the water debts were carried over to the next night and even later into the week. When it became too dark to carry on, I was always glad that the time had come to tell Mimi I had to go home. It was a relief after running on the edge of that much excitement to be back in my own house and safe in my own bed.

Mimi and I stayed outside and sat on the stoop. "Bee-Bee wants to build a bathroom," she told me. "Last night he measured where to put the pipes. He wants to install a pump but he said the bathroom has to be on the bottom floor. He said, '*Mes tantes* can come downstairs to pee.'" She paused. "Pierrette says our stepfather is taking over. She says our mother made a big mistake. Bee-Bee wouldn't even let my mother cut her own hair for their wedding. He wants it long, he said."

We wondered if Mimi's mother would attend Pierrette and Ferdinand's wedding at the end of summer, since Pierrette had snubbed her own. We were pretty sure that Bee-Bee would have the final say.

The caddis flies were plentiful this close to the river and we had to keep brushing them away from our faces. Uncle Henri came out to the stoop and limped down the path towards the outhouse. He had been wounded in the leg the last day of the war and wasn't able to work because there were still pieces of metal lodged in his bones. Henri had come home with a damaged leg *and* a wife; he and his English bride lived in a tiny apartment at the back of the house. The Bride worked alongside one of the aunts at the Metropolitan five-and-dime, in Hull. They were both assigned to the candy counter, and they took turns bringing home banana-shaped candies with soft yellow insides, and licorice pipes with fiery red bowls.

Just as Henri reached the outhouse at the end of the yard, the Bride came to the door and called, "Dah'ling! Dah'ling!" as if to urge him on. Mimi and I hooted with laughter and ran out of the yard. We never tired of listening to the English bride, especially when she talked about the war. During rationing, she'd told us once, a large cardboard box filled with tea had arrived in Bath from Canada. She pronounced the place "Bawth," which we thought remarkable. She and her mother and two of their neighbours had sat at the kitchen table all of one afternoon, tearing tea bags and dumping raw tea leaves into tins. Why would the Canadians, they asked one another over and over again, why would the Canadians go to the bother of sewing tea into tiny bags only to take it out again when they wanted to drink? Henri, too, loved the stories of the Bride, even though he'd been married for eight years and had probably heard them all before.

The sumac trees were high and full along the lower edge of the Pines, their tops linked in broad umbrellas. The birds were in there thickly, we could hear them. And the whisker grass had grown as tall as our knees. Mimi and I walked to the wall and dangled our feet over the rapids and threw in loose chunks of stone. We followed the bank upriver, towards my house. When we passed *the last place of safety — or not —* I pointed it out, although there was nothing to see. It was the place from which Father had drawn an invisible line that began at the chokecherry tree on shore. The line stretched first to the long and narrow Unreachable Island, surrounded by rapids at its lower end. After that, it extended several miles across water into infinity. For us, that was Britannia, in Ontario, on the other side.

Any time we swam in our cove, we were allowed to float down on the current, feet first, but only until our toes crossed the imaginary line. Then we had to stand up, wade to shore and make our way upriver before wading in and floating down again.

Mimi's family lived well below the last place of safety, past the river's curve, and past the end of the rapids. Our family lived above and always had to deal with the possibility of drifting into danger. "If you float past this line," Father never tired of telling us, "you'll never be able to get back." I had tried my luck floating past the line a few times, but never when Father was around. I didn't go too much farther but had never found it difficult to right myself and get back to shore.

"Imagine," said Mimi, "if we stood here and the water

parted and we walked to Unreachable Island. The rapids would hang over our heads and wait for us to get through."

"Imagine," I said, thinking of *Christ walketh on the sea.* "Imagine if we walked on *top* of the water. But if the miracle ended, we'd be surrounded by rapids and we'd die."

"Not if we had faith," said Mimi. "My mother has faith. *Mes tantes* have faith. Not Bee-Bee, though. Bee-Bee doesn't go to Mass."

We talked about Pierrette and Ferdinand, then, the future bride and groom. Did Pierrette have to stand on a chair to kiss her fiancé? Their bodies were clearly mismatched. The subject of the bull came up — Ferdinand, who refused to butt his head like the other bulls. We both liked him, and we teased him, sometimes, about the story of the bull.

"Do your father and mother have birth control?" said Mimi. She caught me off guard.

"I don't know," I said.

"In our church," she said, "the priest doesn't allow." She wasn't sure how he managed this but the numbers of people in her house were proof of his interference. "My father used to say," she said — and she crossed herself the way the Catholics did on the bus whenever they passed a graveyard or a church — "it's the priest's fault and the fault of Monsieur Duplessis."

I knew about Mr. Duplessis but I had never heard my parents talk about birth control. It had not occurred to me that the priest and Monsieur Duplessis and birth control might be connected. It was hard enough to imagine the details of what Mimi said my parents did to each other in bed.

"Like Adam and Eve," she said. "Everybody does it. It's only a sin if you're not married." She added glumly, "My mother and Bee-Bee do it. At night I hear them."

The aunts had not let go of the miracle and continued to discuss it around the big table. Pierrette's role did not seem to be important any more; she'd only reported what she had seen. The woman in the rapids now belonged to everyone. It was as if by repeating every detail, more would be known.

"Her eyes were open."

"Pierrette said so. She can see that far."

"Not me. I can't see my own two feet."

"How long was her hair?"

"Not long, not short."

"It was medium," said Pierrette, from the kitchen counter.

"And dark?"

"Everything was in mist."

"And her hand. You're sure it was the left?"

"I'm sure."

"It was a warning. It has to be."

The aunts sat back in their chairs.

Grand-mère said, "The way grasshoppers spit tobacco, that's a miracle."

They all looked at her. I sneaked a glance at her tiny wrists and thought of my Giant Ant, Aunt Lucy King, who had the big bones.

"A warning," Pierrette said. "Not that kind of miracle, Grand-mère."

The oldest aunt said, "The warning was probably for me — for my sins. I should never have given in to Robert. He wouldn't have left me." She pronounced his name Ro-by-er.

Everyone laughed.

"That was so long ago I'm surprised you remember," said Tante Florence.

"Well, *you* shouldn't walk around upstairs in your brassiere with only a towel over your shoulders when there's a man in the house," the oldest aunt said. "It was probably a warning for you to stay out of trouble."

"Bee-Bee? I'm not worried," said Tante Florence.

Mimi's mother made a face.

Bee-Bee came into the room as if he'd been summoned, and they all clammed up.

A scent of cedar lingered over the upstairs landing of Mimi's big house. Along the railing, hope chests belonging to the aunts were lined up in a row. Pierrette's was there, too, full to the lid and threatening to overflow. One by one the unmarried aunts had been slipping fingers into pressed and folded layers, transferring items from their own hoards over to Pierrette's. No one else had the initial *P* so they did not give up monogrammed pillowcases and sheets, but they parted with satin half-slips and linen tea towels and brightly pastel mules for Pierrette's feet.

There was an alcove on the landing, too. A narrow curtain had been hung from a sawed-off broomstick and behind the curtain were a mirror, a sink with an open drain and a bucket underneath. There was a sink downstairs, too, in the kitchen, a bucket under that. Water was carted continuously into the house, up and down stairs; and slop-water — as Bee-Bee called it — carried back out.

Mimi's mother and the aunts were getting ready to go to a movie at the Laurier Theatre, in Hull, and Mimi and I were sitting on the lid of Pierrette's hope chest as they took turns darting in and out of the alcove in multiple states of undress. Sometimes Mimi and I went to a movie in Ottawa with Lyd on Saturday afternoons but we'd never been to one in Hull, because of the fire. *Seventy-eight children dead: the Laurier Palace, Montreal, January 9, 1927.* We knew the date as well as we knew our own birthdays. It was the date after which no child below the age of sixteen was permitted to attend a movie in the Province of Quebec. We talked about the fire as if it had happened three weeks, and not almost three decades, ago.

"Some of the children were little," said Mimi. "I hope they were baptized."

"They were crushed," I said. "Most of them." I imagined miniature bones trampled by feet.

"Their dresses burned," said Mimi. "Their arms and wrists. Sister showed us a picture in a book. The roof collapsed, and I saw a shoe."

"Their lungs would have filled with smoke first," I said. I was thinking of the drills Father had put us through: *Shout "FIRE! FIRE!" Drop to the floor. Crawl to the nearest window. Meet across the road by the river and stay put. NEVER GO BACK INSIDE.*

"The fire would have been a good time for a miracle," Mimi said. "But it didn't happen. Someone could have appeared and told the children to stay calm. Someone could have led them to the exit. Or two people, maybe."

"Even if they'd just walked through the flames," I said. "If they hadn't run, they'd still be alive. They'd be old now."

"No one knows when a miracle will happen and save someone," said Mimi. "It has to happen by surprise."

I thought of the *five thousand*. Could they have known that they were about to be fed with five loaves and two fishes? Did

Daniel know that God would send an angel to shut the mouths of the lions? You always had to be ready, because something might take place right under your nose and you might miss it.

"What about Monsieur Côté, next door?" I said. "He might wake up suddenly and find out he's had a close brush with communism. That could be a miracle." I'd heard Father say that even your next-door neighbour could be a Communist. He said that what a man hoped for was a house to drive up to where he could park his car at the curb and know his family was safe inside; where he could walk down a street and be greeted by a handshake and the warm touch of an old friend. But we had no car and no curb; only a dirt road. We had no neighbours, either, on chemin Brébeuf, but Mimi did, on her street. She and I had been watching Monsieur Côté ever since the day Father had talked about the Communists.

"Or Madame Chenier, by the bus stop," said Mimi. "Her stomach is as big as a watermelon but there's no baby inside. Everybody says it's a tumour that's so heavy she has to hold it up with her hands when she walks. Maybe she'll wake up one morning and her stomach will be flat."

"You two are morbid," Mimi's mother said. She was wearing a tight skirt with a pleat at the bottom, a thin peach cardigan buttoned down the back. "Pick out my earrings," she said to Mimi and Mimi slid off the hope chest and disappeared into her mother's room.

The aunts came out of their rooms, dressed for the movie and the bus ride to Hull. Mimi returned with white chiclet clip-ons for her mother.

"Don't play outside too late, you two," said Mimi's mother. "Grand-mère is in her room. She wants to sleep. Pierrette's around, I think, and Bee-Bee's here. Anyway, Henri and the Bride are always at the back of the house if you can't find anyone."

It was one of those warm-breath summer evenings. We could hear sounds from far away, and yet everything seemed enclosed. We could have walked from one end of the village to the other and it would have been the same. Heaviness and stillness. Everything stopped. No one behind screen doors making the slightest effort to move. The insides of houses were purposely in shadow; it was too early for lights.

Some of Mimi's friends from her street wandered into the backyard and we soon had enough for hide-and-seek. We determined that the stoop would be home-free and we set out our territory: two yards — front and back — Mimi's and the Côté's; the line of trees; the sheds; the veranda. We chanted *Am-Stram-Gram* and worked our way down to the Côté boy, the only one left. I wondered if he was a little Communist. "You're *it*," we shouted in his face, and scattered. Mimi and I raced past the Bride's English garden and around to the front of the house.

"We should stick together," Mimi said. "Let's go inside. We can sneak upstairs and come down the back way. Quick!"

We opened the screen and tried not to make a noise. Pressed ourselves against the wall when we heard the counting stop, and waited. Mimi pointed at the stairs and gestured at me to run up first. She slipped behind a door as I tiptoed up to the landing. The place seemed deserted, uninhabited, without the aunts coming in and out of their rooms. But Bee-Bee came out of Mimi's mother's room, suddenly, and filled the doorway.

We were both startled but he recovered first. "Hide-and-seek?" he said, and I nodded. "Quick," he said. "In here. I'll hide you."

He opened the door to a room I had never been in. There were two dressers, a large cardboard box, a sofa, a desk and a tiny chair. It might have been a sitting room, or a storeroom for extra furniture. I turned around and saw Mimi, who'd followed me upstairs.

"You'll be safe here," Bee-Bee said. "I'll go down and scout out who's around the stoop and I'll tell you when to run for it." He slipped out of the room and closed the door behind him.

The room was dim; the blind had been pulled and the overhead light was off. I smelled must, old wood; the room was probably never used. A long time seemed to go by. Bee-Bee finally reappeared and said, "Everyone's gone, they must have gotten fed up. Now I have to take you hostage and lead you downstairs."

He had tea towels in one hand and rope in the other. "Turn around," he said.

We hesitated, but shrugged and turned. We'd often played with Bee-Bee, but not like this. He gagged each of us, in turn, and tied the knot at the back of our heads. Mimi and I looked at each other over the gags and tried to laugh.

"Hands behind your backs," he said.

He tied us both at the wrists and told us to lie on the floor on our stomachs. Then he tied our feet up behind us and attached the rope to our bound wrists. He was working slowly, tightening the knots as he moved from one to the other. Mimi and I could barely see each other. The rope was rough and made my wrists uncomfortable when I tried to shift. My arms had begun to ache even though they hadn't been in that position very long. Bee-Bee was breathing quickly, his eyes bright and darting as he checked the ropes. He pulled a loose end tightly between my ankles and my wrists, and pain shot through one of my legs. He was silent, alert, all his attention focused on the way he was tying us, every knot checked and rechecked. I felt tears coming into my eyes but did not want to cry. I tried to see Mimi but she had gone limp and would not look at me.

"There," said Bee-Bee. He stood over us, massive, from where we lay at his feet. He seemed pleased with himself, and excited. "Don't be cowards. You're only hostages for a few minutes. Then I'll come back and let you go." His legs moved away and I heard him leave the room and shut the door.

We waited, but the house was silent. There was no sound from the yard below; the children had gone. I could barely hear the river outside — the fast wash at the end of the rapids. Mimi made noises through her gag. My teeth were biting into the towel and I made a noise in reply. There was nothing we could do. I was tied so securely I couldn't even inch my way along the floor.

He'll come back, I said to myself. It's only a stupid game. He'll come in here and untie us and we'll rub our wrists and ankles and then we'll be free.

I wanted to go home. I had to be back by dark. With the blind down I couldn't tell how late it was. A long time went by. I heard a gasp and tried to turn my head. Bee-Bee was leaning against the door in the shadows. His mouth was open and his eyes were drooped half-closed and his breath was coming out of him in strange bursts. I realized with a sickening lurch in my chest that he'd never left. He looked down at me without saying anything and turned his back and this time he did go out. I watched him pull the door shut behind him. It was impossible to know how long he'd been in the room.

I tried to think where Grand-mère's room was, below. I traced the rooms of the house, upstairs and down, in my head, and realized that it was the front of the house we were in, not the back. Mimi had come to life and was trying to move, trying to roll herself in some awkward way against the chair near her body. I didn't want to cry because Bee-Bee would come back any minute and he would call us babies if we cried, and it would all be a big joke.

But he didn't come back.

I knew my mother and father would be angry. I began to believe that we might never be free. No one would find us and Bee-Bee wouldn't tell anyone where we were. I thought of the stories Georgie-Porgie had told us last New Year's, the ones about old skeletons turning to dust in silent rooms. When someone would finally come and nudge the skeleton with a shoe, the skull, with its empty eye sockets, would fall off.

Maybe Lyd and Eddie would miss me and start looking. They would come to Mimi's big house and demand to go through all the rooms. But Lyd and Eddie would never look for me. Eddie would be reading comics at home, and Lyd would be playing records or reading her new Nancy Drew.

The muscles in my legs had cramped and I had pins and needles in my arms. It was so dark inside now, I could only see the curve of Mimi's body, though I was aware of the warmth of her, in the room.

We heard footsteps on the stairs and someone walking towards the alcove at the end of the hall. Mimi's body made a rolling lunge, knocking over the chair. It fell, resting against the edge of the desk. The overhead light went on and we looked up at Henri's Bride who was blinking at us from the doorway.

"Oh my God," she said. "Oh my God, what's going on? *Dah'ling!*" she called, at the top of her lungs, *"Dah'ling!* Come quick." She ran out of the room and we heard her pounding on a wall. A door opened from the back part of the house and Henri limped along the hallway and stood looking down at us.

It took the two of them ten minutes to cut the rope, to untie us knot by knot, and they were furious. When my limbs were free I found I couldn't stand. I had to rub at my legs and arms and wait until the blood started moving again. Mimi was hiccuping; her whole body was shaking and she couldn't make it stop.

"That fool," said Henri. "He has his nerve touching you like this." He and the Bride exchanged looks.

By this time, Pierrette had come in and they told her what had happened. She led us both downstairs and said, "Where the hell is he? I knew he was a creep the way he looked at me the first time our mother brought him home. And ever since," she added.

She softened when she talked to us and she asked us what he had done.

"He gagged us and tied us up," said Mimi. "He said it was just for fun. We were playing hide-and-seek and he told us the other kids had gone home. He was supposed to come back and untie us but he didn't come back." She did not say that Bee-Bee had stayed in the room.

"He didn't do anything else?"

"No."

"Go on up to the store," she said. "Tell the Bull I said to give you a melorol. Tell him I'll be there later. Hurry up, before it's dark. Trude can go home from the store. Mimi, you wait there with Ferdinand until I come." She put an arm around each of us. "You're okay," she said. "You're not hurt." She looked at Henri and the Bride over our heads and added, "I'm staying right here until I find the S-O-B."

Mimi and I went to the stoop and ran down the steps and out of the yard. We didn't want to bump into Bee-Bee.

"Bee-Bee's in trouble," she said. "Because it wasn't like playing. Pierrette's going to tell our mother, I can tell. Are you going to tell your mother?"

"No," I said, and at that moment I was certain that I never would. It was something to do with my own mother and father; what Mimi told me they did. It was Mother's face, sometimes, after I'd heard her and father argue behind their closed door; her red-rimmed eyes, a look as if something were missing, as if we were not enough for her, as if she already had some sorrow of her own.

And it was remembering Bee-Bee's face, above us, when he'd been leaning into the door while Mimi and I were lying on the floor. The knowledge that he'd been in the room with us for a long time and we hadn't known. *That* was worse than being tied up. All of this together, I knew I would not be able to describe or explain.

When we reached the end of the street and headed up rue Principale, we slowed to a walk. The sun had begun to set and the nine o'clock curfew would soon sound from the Catholic school. We looked back in the direction of the river. We were still rubbing at our wrists, at the faint streaks of red that had been left by the rope.

"My mother says, 'Smile if it kills you,'" I said, and we both forced a terrible smile.

"Maybe the woman in the rapids was giving a warning, after all," said Mimi. "A warning about *le beau-père*, the stepfather. We'll never get a bathroom now, if everyone's mad."

Just then we paused and tilted our heads. Flocks of purple martins preparing to settle for the night had begun to swing over us like dark nets in the sky. In the distance, they rose and fell and rose again. And then, we watched their sudden singular descent as they vanished remarkably and all at once into the clump of trees beyond our cove. We waited until we were sure they would not rise again and we continued on to the new store owned by Ferdinand the Bull. This time, however, we did not call out as we did on other evenings, vying for the sighting of the birds, hoping to be the first to shout out: *"My wedding! My wedding!"*

SISTERS

1953

"A boy after Mass," Mimi said — it was her turn with the oar — "told me the nuns bury dead babies behind the convent, in the woods."

"That's where we pick dogtooth violets for Mother's Day," I said.

"The boy made it up," said Mimi. "It isn't true. It's a sin to say that."

I thought of the nuns, their long sweeping skirts and half-hidden enamel faces. Unlike the priest, they were rarely sighted in the village. I did not know where they bought their groceries or what kind of food they ate.

"The nuns are married to Jesus," said Mimi. She preened while she said this.

But the way she thought of the nuns was the way I thought

of her and of all the Catholic girls in the village: child brides of Christ. An army of them marching forward, starting their journey under flowing white veils from the time of their First Communion — from the day they accepted the gift of the white rosary. To me they were a separate order of marked children bearing the weight of the Sorrowful Mysteries, bearing the weight of the Faith.

"Anyway," Mimi said, "the nuns are good teachers. But when Sister gets mad she cuffs us on the back of the head with her hand. She sneaks up behind us and sprinkles water on the back of our necks."

We thought about this for a moment.

"If it's true about the dead babies," Mimi said, "I wonder if they're baptized before they die. If they aren't, they stay in limbo."

"It wouldn't be the same if the baby was born in a house with a mother and father," I said. "Still, if the baby died, the mother and father would go mad with the grief." *The grief* was what Granny Tracks sometimes talked about when she told us about Grandfather Meagher.

"Limbo is where the baby would go if it isn't baptized," Mimi said. "It would have to stay in limbo for a long time. It might never get all the way to heaven. The priest said."

I tried to think of a layer of babies in gowns, all trying to get closer to heaven. It was hard to imagine. Instead, I saw rows of little boxes buried in the woods.

Mimi handed me the oar and I turned it end to end and we changed places. The boat was tied and we pushed it back and forth in an arc, drooping our hands over the sides, our fingers darting after crayfish that slipped under the rocks. We stayed in the boat because Mimi was wearing her Sunday shoes with the black patent straps and had been told not to go into the river. She kept her feet on the wooden platform in the bottom of the boat. There was always water beneath the platform — water that could never be bailed.

I had changed as soon as I'd come home on the bus. I'd been to Hull for Sunday school and church, and today had added a new Bible card to my collection: *Job sheweth the wicked may prosper*. I'd been thinking about the wicked when I'd gone up the church basement stairs and slipped into the pew beside Mother and Lyd. Eddie had stayed in the basement to be supervised, below, while we were in church.

The wicked were all around us, we'd been told, and I thought that perhaps this was like communism. I looked at the Anglicans, their light summer coats pressed shoulder to shoulder in the pews ahead. I'd been forced to wear a hat to church, a crescent-shaped hat with a veil that tugged over my eyes. I hated the hat. The veil scratched my forehead and obstructed my vision. But it had to be worn. I looked through it at Lyd and Mother beside me, and when Mother looked back and raised an eyebrow, I slipped off the seat and kneeled on the hard planks of wood that flipped out from under the pew ahead. I tried to think of a prayer. Mother and Lyd always closed their eyes as if they knew in advance exactly what they were going to pray.

I looked straight ahead and then up at the ceiling, where a ribboned banner had been painted onto the arch of the church. I read silently: *I was glad when they said unto me. Let us go into the house of the Lord.* I thought about being glad. The bells were ringing in the tower and the vibrations shivered through the seat and behind me and above. Before I said a prayer I pictured the street outside, the tiny portion of the

main street of Hull. People unknown to me would be pausing
and looking up. They would have no way of knowing that I
was here inside, listening to the call of the bells. Surrounded
by and pulled into the heaviness of oak and deep stone.

Every night I said, "Now I lay me down to sleep," and
prayed for my entire family. "God bless Mother, Father, Lyd,
Eddie, Granny Tracks, Uncle Weylin, Aunt Arra and Georgie-
Porgie, Grampa King and everyone at the King farm, also the
orphans and the poor and my best friend, Mimi." In church I
decided to use the same prayer but this time I left out the *Now
I lay me* part.

After the choir sailed by I cast my attention to the stained-
glass window on my right. Jesus was there, the same likeness
that was on my Bible cards. The milky glass made Him look
as if He were already dead. He was meant to be alive though,
because He was beckoning to a circle of little children dressed
in cream-coloured tunics. Two of the disciples were trying to
turn the children away but this did not please Him. The words
in the window read: *Suffer the little children to come unto me.*
Not one of the children with cropped black hair looked
anything like any child I'd ever seen, in St. Pierre or in Hull.

Mimi had brought licorice pipes to the boat and we sucked on
these while we pushed each other back and forth. I knew that
nothing I could conjure would ever compete with Mimi's
Catholic underworld — peopled with sinners and confessors
and the constant threat of terror. Her sisters, she told me, had
always made things up when they went to confession so
they'd have something to tell the priest. Except for the time
they'd put on new brassieres and walked to the corner bus

stop and paraded past the driver when he had to turn the empty bus around and head back to Hull. "The driver's face was beet red," they told Mimi. That time, they'd all confessed the truth to the priest.

In my church, the Anglicans I'd watched that morning — except for a girl who had one brown eye and one blue — were insipid by comparison. I had stared into the face of the girl with the mismatched eyes so I could tell Mimi about her, later.

"In my family, everyone has hazel eyes," Mimi said now. "Every single one. They aren't green and they aren't blue. They're somewhere in between. Except Bee-Bee," she said. "But he's not part of our real family. Anyway, he's gone again."

Bee-Bee had disappeared for weeks and then turned up and moved back into her mother's bedroom. Pierrette had been furious that their mother had taken him back. I had not visited when Bee-Bee was there; Mimi had come to my house, or we'd waited until the coast was clear. Mother didn't seem to notice that we were hanging around our place more. Now Bee-Bee was gone again.

"I know a song about the Sisters," Mimi said. "I can teach you in English and French. We call it 'Back of My Auntie's House.'"

> If you become a nun,
> Nun in a convent ground,
> I'll turn to preacher then
> And preaching will you hound.

> *Si tu te mets prêcheur*
> *Pour m'avoir en prêchant,*
> *Je me donn'rai à toi*
> *Puisque tu m'aimes tant!*

I spotted a flash in the water and dug in the oar to steady the boat. I handed the oar to Mimi. "Hold it there," I said. "I see something." I shoved a rock aside and lifted my prize from the river.

I shook the water from a string of brown and bloated chunky beads from which a tiny cross hung straight down. It was the first rosary I'd ever held in my hands.

"*Mon Dieu*," said Mimi. "If you lose your beads, you lose your luck." She added grimly, "Maybe somebody threw them in."

I leaned over the boat and washed every wooden bead and then I carried them up to the house. Mimi showed me the Hail Mary beads and the Glory Be bead but she did not want to handle them herself.

"They could keep us safe," I said. "We could make things up to say over each one."

But Mimi had her own white beads, and she did not want to say anything over these.

Lyd was the only one in the house when we went in. She was standing in front of Duffy's long mirror. Lyd was the tallest girl in her class at school and at Sunday school. Because she would soon be thirteen, this was the cut-off year for her to leave Stone and start Brick. We'd still be taking the same orange bus out of the village but we'd be going to different schools. We knew that the one-room schools would be pooled together in a *new* school, but before that could happen the new school had to be built.

"All I did at Sunday school was pass out animal crackers to

the little kids," Lyd said. "I get claustrophobic on that stage. I don't know why they close the curtains."

"It's just babysitting," I said. "Don't you give them Bible pictures to colour?"

"I did," she said. "Moses in the bulrushes. And while they were crunching their little brown camels I closed my eyes and prayed to God to keep my feet from growing as quickly as my height." She snorted.

The last time Father measured us, Lyd's mark had jumped an inch and a half on the pantry door. We both knew there were genes in the family to be reckoned with — the genes of our Giant Ant, Aunt Lucy King. The two of us were always on the lookout for women with wide shoulders and huge bones. We were on the lookout for Big Feet. We knew that a wild and erratic gene might already have skipped, Amazon-like, into our own bones. I remembered Aunt Lucy in Darley, hooting with laughter as she held up one of her own size-twelve feet.

"Where *is* everybody?" I said.

"Mother and Father are at Rebecque's," she said. "Duffy stays at her place overnight now, but he can't marry her because his runaway wife won't give him a divorce. Anyway, the Church won't allow. Eddie's playing in the Pines with his friends. He's trying to prove that Brébeuf was tortured at the top of our road, where it turns into chemin Brébeuf."

"Brébeuf wasn't killed anywhere near here," I said. "He only canoed past. We studied him in school. He died some-where in Ontario."

"Try to tell that to Eddie," she said.

I showed Lyd the rosary. The circle of it was large and she slipped it over her head and draped it around her neck. Then she went to the window and checked the path through the field to see if anyone was coming. She began to take off her clothes one by one in front of the mirror. Mimi and I stared. Only the rosary was around Lyd's neck. It lay heavily over her tanned bare skin.

"Somebody might come in," I said. I didn't know why she was doing this.

"They'll be a while," she said. She was scrutinizing the new patch of hair, the height of her leg bones, the length of her feet. She stretched her neck and lifted the rosary and turned sideways to examine her breasts. Mimi and I looked at each other; she and I still played outside, sometimes, with our shirts off, but Lyd could never do that now.

"I checked Mother's name book," she said. "I looked up my name to see what it stands for. Lyd means *the voluptuous one*." She scrambled back into her clothes. "I hate my arms," she said. "There's dark hair on my arms. And I don't have my period yet. It's taking forever. I'll be getting it this year, I'll bet. And when I start, I'm going to call it *Jennifer*. That's what girls call their periods when they talk about them so no one else will know. You two are babies," she said. "You don't have to worry about this yet."

Mimi and I went to Mother's sewing bench where the name book was kept. We looked up the girls' section and found Trude, which was from *Gertrude* and meant *spear-loved maiden*. The name made me feel fierce. Mimi was from *Mary* so we looked up *Mary*, which meant *bitter*. I wanted to know what Mother's name meant, too, so I looked up Maura, which was from *the Moor,* and meant *the dark one*.

"Look up *Jennifer*," said Lyd.

But all we could find under *Jennifer* was *"See Guinevere,"* and *Guinevere* meant *white*.

"It's a disguise for *red*," Lyd said. "That's why periods are called *Jennifer*. It's the perfect disguise." She took off the rosary and handed it back to me and we returned the name book to the sewing bench.

I went into the bathroom and examined the stubby bottles of nail polish lined up on the bathroom shelf. Sometimes Mother let us borrow one so we could paint our toenails while we sat by the river in the sun.

I chose Siren Red and carried it out to the lilacs in the backyard. Mimi and I crouched in the shade while I painted the river-swollen beads, one by one. When they were dry, I slipped them over my head and hid the cross at the back of my neck. We headed for the front of the house.

"No one will ever know," I told Mimi. "It's a new necklace I found. A necklace with powers."

But while I'd been painting the beads Father and Mother had returned and Father was slumped into his canvas chair in the front yard. He squinted against the sun and spotted the necklace right away.

"Off!" he yelled. "Get the damned thing off!" He pointed to my neck and shouted again. "Take it off and throw it away!"

"I found it," I said. "It's mine. I found it in the river."

"Then you just throw it right back in, young lady. Now."

Mimi cast a baleful look in Father's direction and we headed down to the river. As we did, I heard Father mutter, "Damned mumbo-jumbo," and I said to myself, "The beads must give him what Granny Tracks calls the heebie-jeebies."

When we reached shore I took off my Siren Red beads and pretended to throw them into the water. Instead, I kept them in my palm. I turned to see if Father was watching but he was not. He'd left his canvas chair and had gone into the house. Probably to tell Mother.

"He's going to kill you if you keep them," said Mimi.

"Quick!" I said. "Come on." I led her farther downriver and squatted beside the chokecherry tree. I broke off a piece of shale and dug into the earth at the base of the tree. I scraped a hole six inches deep and lowered the beads into it and filled the hole with dirt. Then I raked the dirt with a twig and spread dried leaves over the top and marked the cache with a tiny scroll of bark. I walked ten paces away from the river and took my bearings. I memorized the line-up of trees and the formation of shale. Just beyond the cache there was a giant maple, the one that threw a wide shadow at dusk. When we ran through the shadow we had to hold our breath. If we breathed while we were still in shadow, the curse of Brébeuf would be upon us. We would feel hands around our throat and we would choke. I had never breathed in the shadow.

"Never mind," I said to Mimi. "We'll always know where the rosary is and we can dig it up when we need it. No one will ever find it. It's too well disguised."

We kept on walking, up through the Pines, past the cliff and the high wild rapids and the old hydro wall. Logs were jammed like pick-up sticks against the wall and waves rushed around them as if they were beating their way through. When we got to Mimi's house, we found Grand-mère in the kitchen.

"We'll be going on our holidays soon," I told her. "Back to Ontario. My Giant Ant always wants to know everything. She makes me sit on a chair and she says, 'Talk French!' I have to say: *'Comment allez-vous? Quel dommage! Il a un chien. Il s'appelle Pitou.'*"

Grand-mère laughed with delight.

"That's good," said Mimi. "If you keep saying the same things over and over, your big auntie won't know the difference."

When we went upstairs, Mimi's Tante Florence was at the Singer, pumping the pedal. She was feeding a long panel of material that looked like crêpe under the bobbing needle. The day after the King had died, one of Lyd's classmates had carried in a picture of him, framed and edged in the same kind of black crêpe. Lyd had a picture in her Royal scrapbook of the Princess at the door of a plane. She was in deep mourning, the caption said. Even before she'd returned to England, the world had known that she was already Queen.

"I'm making a black dress for Tante Noelle," Tante Florence told Mimi. She turned to me. "Noelle is our one sister who can't sew worth a damn. She heard a rumour that the Pope is sick, and she wants to be ready. He's seventy-eight this year," she said, and she crossed herself.

Mimi and I sat on a hope chest and cross-clapped our hands.

> One's joy
> Two's grief
> Three's a wedding
> Four's death!

On my way home I walked the long way and headed through the village and up into the woods. I was careful not to trespass on the priest's property beside the church. The two-storey Catholic school was beside it, a black fire escape spidering up the side. Set back into the woods was the convent, which I skirted and came at from behind. I scuffed my feet along the main path, where I knew the Sisters walked, and I kept watch. I was completely hidden by trees.

I knew that I would have to look for twigs and branches spread over a larger cache. I scanned every bit of dirt around and between trees and then I left the path and searched and searched but could find no sign that anything had been disturbed. There were no tiny mounds, no splinters of wood from hastily nailed-together boxes, nothing that I could tell of attempts to disguise the patterns of earth. I was both disappointed and relieved but told myself that I might come back to look, another time. I left the shade and shadow of the woods, being careful not to be seen from the convent windows, and I walked slowly home.

When I sat down for supper, Mother brought a platter of pickerel and another of French fries to the table. She always made the fries at the last minute so they'd be fresh, and now she scooped a sieveful out of the hot oil and dumped them onto the brown paper she'd layered on the oven door. She threw in another handful of potatoes and the oil flared up and sizzled and spattered. This was my favourite meal.

"Where did you and Mimi go?" said Mother.

"Nowhere," I said.

We bowed our heads and Mother perched on the edge of her chair so she could get up again to check the fries. Father intoned from the head of the table:

> Be present at our table Lord
> Be here and everywhere adored

These creatures bless and grant that we
May feast in paradise with Thee.

"Amen," we all said together.

I opened my eyes. Mother passed the ketchup to the end of the table and Father thumped the bottom of the bottle with his palm. A splurt of red blurped out onto his plate. Lyd and I exchanged looks.

"Jennifer," her lips mouthed.

Eddie picked up the bottle and *he* thumped it too. I thought of how he would never be a part of what Lyd and I would have to go through.

Lyd looked at the red blob on Eddie's plate and made a face. I tried not to laugh. I was still mad at Father for forcing me to get rid of the rosary.

"*Blood*," I said to myself. Lyd is waiting for blood to come out of her and after it happens to her it's going to happen to me. We'll be forced to wear lumpy pads between our legs like the ones in the box in the bathroom cupboard, and everything will be a huge mess. A red mess, I thought. *Siren Red*.

I looked at Mother and I knew then that there were things she knew that she had never told us. *Dark*, I thought. *The Moor*. Mother knew about periods and she knew about having babies and she never talked to us about either.

Then I remembered the name book and *spear-loved maiden*, and I felt fierce again. I thought of my beads coiled in the cavity of dirt beside the river. I looked at Father and said to myself: "Whenever I want to, I'll go right back to shore and dig up the rosary. I'll dig it up and I'll run each painted bead through my fingers. Not right away but when I need to, so I'll be ready for whatever happens in my life. For whatever tries to take me by surprise."

SPIRIT SPIDERS

1954

Lyd insisted that she could hear spiders, and the apparent truth of this caused me anxiety whenever she claimed one was in the room. Certainly, during the summers, the porch housed its share. But we'd be sitting in the living room or the kitchen and she'd announce in a sing-song voice, "There's one in here," and Eddie and I would freeze position and scan ceiling and walls. Of course there would be a spider. A big grey one looming high on the wall over someone's head. Living that close to the river, there was always a fat spider looming.

"Spirit spiders." That's what Lyd called the ones she could hear. "It's speaking to me," she'd say. "Someone just crawled up from the dead."

Just as there were spiders in our porch in St. Pierre, there were plenty of spiders at Grampa King's farm in Ontario, three miles out of Darley. Granny Tracks, on Mother's side, lived in town. When we made our annual train trip during the summer of 1954, we slept at the King farm, as always. There were more beds at the farm for the five of us. We visited Granny Tracks for day visits, town visits. Occasionally, Mother stayed overnight in town, and Father borrowed Grampa King's Ford to pick her up and bring her back the next day.

I loved being at the farm, outside of Darley. Each morning I rose with the rooster's crow and raised the blind to stare straight across at the stone barn, with its tufts of hay protruding from the open haymow. I looked down to the dirt yard below, where hens were already scratching about, and listened closely, hoping that no one else was up before me. There were curtains across the entrances to each of the bedrooms, and I tiptoed past these to make my way downstairs. I had to go through the dining room and down another step and into the long kitchen, past the stove with its water reservoir and the shelf where the sad-irons were kept, and let myself out through the screen door. I walked over to the milkhouse, which smelled of old and fresh milk, sweet and sour mixed, and hoisted myself up to the open platform and sat, waiting, until the others were up. Sometimes, I tried to spot the turkeys, which were temperamental and seemed to lie in wait just so they could chase me.

At the end of Grampa's dusty lane, the railway tracks ran parallel to the gravel road. The roundhouse, with its indoor turntable and monstrous engines, was another half-mile past the end of the lane. Every day at noon, no matter where I was, I listened for the roundhouse whistle.

We had no grandmother at the farm because Grandma King had died before any of us was born. There was only one photo of her, and in that photo the camera had cut her off at the knees. A kindness, Aunt Lucy said, because of the size of Grandma's feet. Our father denied the long-foot story and said that his sister Lucy was full of it. The reason there was only one photo of Grandma King was because she'd had a goitre protruding from her neck.

"She ran from the camera all her life," said Father. "Her feet were absolutely normal. Lucy turned into a giant on her own steam."

It was true that Aunt Lucy had inherited the long-foot gene. She knew we called her the Giant Ant but this didn't bother her one bit. She had even managed to find a husband taller than herself, Uncle Wash.

Lyd said it would take a miracle to unravel the family history. If Grandma King had had a goitre, why had the camera cut her off at the knees instead of the head?

I gave up on all of them and hoped I'd inherited the genes of my mother's side, the Meaghers. They, at least, had managed to contain their growth.

There was work to be done on the farm and Father pitched in as if he'd never left. His younger brother, Ewart, had not married, and lived a bachelor existence with Grampa King. Aunt Lucy, older and taller than both Uncle Ewart and Father, came over most days from her own farm, to help out with the meals.

Sometimes, relations from both sides of the family mixed in, but this happened only at the farm and not often, perhaps because it wasn't a smooth mix. One Sunday, Mother's brother, Uncle Weylin, Aunt Arra and our cousin Georgie drove out from town, bringing Granny Tracks. Everyone shook hands, starting off in the seldom-used parlour where we all stared at the white and black knobs of the organ. I kept glancing at my uncle, trying to merge his face with the story Georgie had told us a year and a half ago, at New Year's. Georgie had been sent to us because his father had chased his mother around the house with a butcher knife. At least Uncle Weylin hadn't killed her, I thought. Aunt Arra was sitting right there beside him in the silent parlour.

After a few minutes we moved rapidly to the kitchen and sat around the long wooden table Grampa King had made. A pot of tea was set at each end.

"Save those honey pails," Granny Tracks said, seeing three of them lined up on the kitchen counter. "Fill them with tea, almost to boiling. Carry them out to the fields when you're working, the hottest time of day." She paused to fold her arms across her chest. "Your body heat will rise to the outdoor temperature," she said. "You'll be so comfortable you'll think you're in the shade."

"What the hell is she talking about?" Grampa King said, looking at Ewart, looking at Father, knowing Granny Tracks had never lived on a farm. But Granny didn't hear, and Mother smoothed things over while our Giant Ant loomed over each of the Meaghers with a plate of cake and fresh tea to "hot up the cups."

These were clearly two separate worlds and the way we behaved in one was not the way we behaved in the other. To make matters worse, Lyd sang out, "There's one in here," and we started giggling, looking around for spirit spiders. The adults didn't know what we were up to and ignored us. We knew that if we couldn't stop giggling, we'd be sent outside, the punishment for rudeness. Which was fine with us.

There was a hired hand on the farm, too. Lorne didn't have

one extra word to spare. He and Grampa King and Uncle Ewart moved in and out of the farmhouse abruptly, making brief, almost wordless exchanges. Eddie, encompassed by their male silence, tagged after them, mute. When the men spoke to Lyd and me, what they said came out as a kind of gruff joke; it was hard to tell whether they were fooling or not.

For a brief period, Father became one of these men. We didn't have to listen to poetry at the farm; we didn't have to march to Tennyson or do quizzes or mental arithmetic; the barometer was not mentioned. Father bottled his deluge and released it only when he got us back to the river, back to Quebec.

Mother still sang her songs to us at the farm, but softly, in the kitchen, when no one else was around. Grampa King's radio was kept in the parlour, beside his chair, and Mother rarely turned it on. Only late Sunday afternoon did everyone sit together with Grampa — Lyd and Eddie and I on the floor — while he and Uncle Ewart and Lorne listened to their favourite program, "Jake and the Kid."

I liked the hired hand. He was the same height as Lyd but square and stocky; he was always staring down at his feet or at the ground. When drinking water was needed, he hooked the stoneboat to the tractor and let me stand on the back where I hung on to the big drums. He dragged me halfway down the dirt lane as far as the spring, speeding the tractor to make sure I could feel every rock through the vibrating soles of my feet. He looked around for me when it was time to throw slop to Grampa's two pigs. He shielded me from assault by the rooster and threw a milkpail over its flapping body, giving me time to escape. He said to me once, "What a man can't keep in his head, he has to make up for with his feet." He stared at the ground. I wasn't sure what this meant. He knew I scratched start- and finish-lines in the dirt of the farmyard and raced against Lyd's unbeatable legs; he lent Eddie his watch with the second hand so Eddie could clock our times. The only way I ever managed to beat Lyd was to run the bare foot race across the stones along the river-bank at home. But I never stopped trying.

"A blind hog," Lorne went on, "sometimes finds an acorn." I thought of Grampa's two pigs shoving against each other's sides, grunting and snorting in the mud. What was Lorne talking about? He never added a word of explanation. "Forget it," Lyd said, "even Lorne doesn't know."

But Lorne connected somehow with Granny Tracks. He'd joined us for tea when the Meagher and King families merged for that brief afternoon at the farm. Lorne was buttering a piece of bread to go with his tea, and dropped his knife on the floor. Both he and Granny Tracks jerked upright in their chairs. "A man is coming," they said in split-breath harmony. For a moment I thought they would lean forward and link little fingers and chant: *What goes up the chimney? Smoke! May your wish and my wish never be broke!*

Lyd and I looked at each other and slipped away from the table, gasping for breath when we got outside. Eddie and Georgie were left snorting, in trouble already for laughing. Nonetheless, the rest of the day, we kept watch over the end of the lane, expecting the arrival of a stranger. When a cloud of dust appeared, we rose to our feet. A car drove up but it was only Uncle Wash, the husband of our Giant Ant, come to collect her as he did every evening, to take her home. Still, *a man came.*

We had ten days left on the farm when Lorne invited Lyd and me for a drive in Grampa's Ford. He was taking salt to the cows, four miles along gravel road, in a field used for grazing. We drove in silence, Lyd and I sitting up front, the windows open, wind blowing through the car. Lorne parked on the shoulder and opened the trunk. Inside were two blocks of salt, each a deep thrilling blue. He stumbled with them one at a time down the embankment and across the dry ditch, and set them close to the fence. He climbed over and pulled a cube through from below. Two cows sauntered near from the side of the field. Lorne headed towards the main herd and told us to wait in the car.

As soon as he was away from us, Lyd challenged. "I bet you can't drive this car."

"I can so," I said. But I knew I couldn't.

"I dare you to try."

"I don't have the key. Lorne took it with him."

"Use a bobby pin," she said. "I'll bet you wouldn't dare."

I never used bobby pins, but in an effort to look older Lyd had recently begun to wear her hair pulled back in a roll, *the Spanish look*. Her head was full of pins.

I straightened the pin and made a loop. "This will never work," I said. "A bobby pin isn't anything like a key." I kept trying, aware of my disloyalty to Lorne. I'd slid behind the wheel but my feet did not entirely reach the floor. I looked back over my shoulder, hoping Lorne would return. He'd delivered one of the blocks and seemed small from where he was, far off by the creek where the cows were drinking and stupidly bumping one another.

I jiggled the pin, pulling knobs I'd seen Lorne pull, and pumping pedals. This was not unlike pumping the organ in Grampa King's living room. The car choked and lunged forward. Lyd and I both shouted.

"You stupid jerk!" she yelled. "You're going to kill us."

The car was lurching forward and I steered it away from the ditch and up onto the gravel. I heard Lorne yell, even from that distance, even above the roar of the Ford. I kept steering because I didn't know how to stop. We were moving right down the middle of the road.

"He's running," Lyd said, in her sing-song voice. "He's almost at the fence."

A steady pitch of curses followed the car. I didn't know how to slow down.

"He jumped over the fence," Lyd said. "Jesus Cripes, you should have seen him."

Lorne's moving torso suddenly filled the open window and I heard him gasping. "Hit the brake! Move your foot hard, hit the one in the middle!"

His arms were through the window and he was helping me steer as he ran alongside. At the same time, he was trying to get the door open.

The car stopped. Died in the silence. I looked up at Lorne and saw his mouth moving, the anger knotted in his face. He heaved the door open as if he were throwing it away.

"You want to drive the goddamned car," he said, "you'll drive 'er." He walked around to Lyd's side and ordered her into the back.

"I don't know how to drive," I said.

"You'll drive the goddamned car," he said again.

I had never heard Lorne swear.

My body all at once became small. I did not think I'd be able to see out the windshield, but of course I could; I'd been steering almost half a mile.

Lorne took the key out of his pocket and handed it over. He

flung Lyd's bobby pin into the ditch. I looked to Lyd for support but she was furious about being ordered into the back, and turned away to stare out the window. I tried to concentrate as I listened to Lorne's instructions but all I could think was, I'm driving this piece of machinery and Lyd is in the back seat and Lorne is forcing me to be in charge of this car. I thought of Mona in our village of St. Pierre, her little feet pushing the pedals of Roy's big car. If Mona could do it, I could do it. I was practically bigger than she was even though she was older than my mother. I pulled out the choke and turned the key and placed my feet on the pedals, feeling them resist and then yield. Lorne talked continuously in my ear. I shifted gears and jerked the car again and again. He kept on talking while I got it going smoothly. He had probably never used so many words.

Only after I veered off the gravel road at Grampa's turn-off without taking us into the ditch did Lorne remember to be silent again. I felt his silence fall around me and this gave me as much strength as his talking. I gripped the wheel and kept my foot evenly on the pedal and I steered the Ford, like a winning chariot, up my Grampa's lane.

Everyone was standing outside the back screen when I braked and jerked the car to a halt: Grampa King, Uncle Ewart, Eddie, our parents, the Giant Ant. I knew that I was in trouble.

But Mother was in a hurry. "Pack your bag," she said. "I've been waiting for you and Lyd. Granny's had a dizzy spell and we're going to town for a few days. Eddie and your father will stay here at the farm.

She was wearing her navy town dress and her hair was in a roll. She was preoccupied and didn't seem to notice that I'd stepped out of the driver's seat. Eddie raised his eyebrows in appreciation. Father, in one of his rare gestures of support, put his hand on Mother's shoulder but she shrugged it off. Grampa King had seen me drive, I knew that. But he chose to remain silent, maybe knowing that Lorne had already handled whatever there was to handle. Lorne stomped off to the barn.

Granny Tracks lived in a narrow two-storey grey house that I thought of as the hollyhock house. There was a fence that bordered an embankment behind the garden and, higher still, trains chuffed by, passing in and out of Darley night and day.

It was possible to stand inside Granny's indoor veranda and touch opposite walls at the same time. The sidewalk ran so close, when people passed by outside, their feet seemed to be walking through the house. Brown linoleum sloped across the floor towards the street. The windowpanes had tiny sashes, like doll windows. The stairs to the second floor led off the kitchen; Granny called them her tower stairs. They were so steep we could make ourselves dizzy by running up as fast as we could, hoping to pass out at the top.

Apart from Granny's room, there was only one other bedroom and this contained two single beds. As Granny Tracks was not used to sleeping with anyone, not in all the long years of *the grief* since Grandfather Meagher had died, she said that she and Mother would have the single beds. Lyd and I were to share the double in her room, a big gloomy room at the front of the house.

Mother argued for sleeping on the couch downstairs but Granny argued back. "I want you in the same room with me," she said. "I always get up in the night. I swear I'm going to tumble down the tower stairs. My time is coming and I'm doomed to die of dizziness. Falling down the stairs your own father refused to put a banister beside. God save his soul," she added.

Mother gave in but she wasn't happy about sleeping upstairs. She helped Granny to the back bedroom, and Lyd and I changed the linen on the big bed where we were to sleep. Lyd paused as we billowed the top sheet. She tilted her head.

"Don't start in on the spiders," I told her. I knew all the signs. My knees had just now begun to shake from driving Grampa's Ford. I was realizing what I had done; remembering Lorne's anger. An image of his short legs running alongside the car as I peered up at his face kept replaying in my mind. I knew Lyd wasn't happy about the way things had turned out — that I'd driven the car for real. Still, a part of me was glowing with triumph.

Granny got up in the night and did not fall down the tower stairs. The next day she refused to leave her bed. She began to run a fever and Mother sent for Dr. Church. He arrived and squeezed his large old body through the doorway. He was the same age as Granny Tracks. They'd been in Darley Public School together from grade one, and Queen Victoria High. After that, Dr. Church had left for medical school in Toronto. Both he and Granny pronounced this "Ter-onna."

"Come on, Mary Meagher," he said. "Get up out of that bed and tell me what's wrong."

"Mind your p's and q's, Randall Church," Granny told him. "It's time for me to die. Can't you tell when a woman's finished living her life?" She scrunched into her pillow as if that might help her disappear.

"You're about as ready to die as I am, Mary Meagher," Dr. Church said. He seemed peeved and irritated, as if they'd done battle before and he'd remembered that he always lost. He stuck his thermometer under her tongue but Granny pulled it out when she saw Lyd and me in the doorway. She held it as though it might get away from her and fly through the air.

"What are you two gawking at?" she said. "Cover that mirror unless you want me staring back at you after I'm dead." She added, almost petulantly, "My spirit will get tangled up when it tries to leave the room." She sounded sick of the whole business, and turned her face to the wall.

Dr. Church spoke to Mother downstairs. Granny did have a fever but he wasn't sure what was wrong. He'd listened to her chest and thought she might be getting pneumonia. Summer pneumonia. Mother was to coax fluids into her, as much as Granny would drink. Dr. Church stopped at the sink on his way through the kitchen and ran his own drink of tap water before he squeezed back through the doorway.

In Granny's room that night I listened as a train chugged past. Vibrations trembled through the metal of our grandparents' bed. After that, silence.

"There's one in here," Lyd sang out in a half-whisper.

"Cut it out, Lyd. I'm trying to sleep. You're making it up, anyway. The whole thing is a joke."

"It's a spirit spider," she said. Her voice was enormously calm.

I didn't respond. But I lay on my back with my eyes open and tried to peer at the corners of the ceiling through the dark.

"It's probably Grandfather Meagher."

"You're going to get it," I said. It was the worst threat I could think of. It was our last-resort threat, though it was meaningless.

"I'll bet fifty dollars there's one in here," Lyd said.

"I don't have fifty dollars and neither do you." Lyd didn't have thirty-nine cents, the price of a Tangee lipstick she'd hoped to buy and secret away that afternoon. We'd walked down Main Street to the Metropolitan and had slashed samples across the inside of our wrists. Lyd liked Tangee because it was what Mother wore; it was supposed to take on the colour of your lips — *one colour suits all.*

"I'll bet you five cents then," Lyd said. "I know there's a spider; I can hear it in the windowsill."

"Okay. Five cents. If you swear you didn't see one before we went to bed."

"Cross my heart and spit. Listen! I hear it now, crawling up from the dead."

I slipped barefoot to the floor and tiptoed to the window. Lyd stood at the light switch, ready to flick it on and off.

As soon as the room flashed to brightness, I shifted the blind. A tiny metallic-looking spider darted under the sash. The light went out.

"Well?"

"That little thing wasn't Grandfather Meagher."

"He probably surfaced from the grave to see how Granny's doing." She turned her back to me and taunted: "You owe me five cents."

Granny Tracks was delirious the next day. Uncle Weylin and Aunt Arra drove over from their home to see what they could do. Dr. Church came back and there was consultation about moving Granny to hospital. For now, everyone agreed, she'd be kept at home until she was free of the fever. But Mother, who'd been up all night, was tired and worried.

We sat with Granny part of the morning while Mother tried to sleep.

"The bricks, the bricks," Granny called out. She was looking our way but didn't seem to see us. "Stack them on the road." Her voice cracked. "Can't you hear what I'm telling you?" Clumps of grey hair had become matted and were sticking straight out, revealing bare patches on a scalp spun with arteries.

She was calm in the evening and Mother persuaded her to take some chicken broth through a straw. But that night and all the next day she was back into delirium.

The entire hollyhock house reeked of onion plaster and camphorated oil. There was no escaping it. Layers of odour rose and sank, clinging to our bodies, upstairs and down. Mother had been weeping in the kitchen over onions that she'd sliced and sautéed and mixed with vinegar and hot mustard. While I watched, she warmed the camphorated oil and spread the mixture across large squares of torn sheet. As she worked, she kept on crying. When the onions were spread evenly, she darned the squares of sheet together with yarn. The finished remedy looked like soggy cloth sandwiches. Two of these were flattened across and then peeled away from Granny's chest and back, every twelve hours.

We tried to get Granny to suck ice chips and we rolled her over and put a strip of rubber sheet under the onion plasters and rolled her back again.

I was trying to help Mother as much as I could but she seemed distant. Filled with a sorrow that could not be reached. We were all worried about Granny but there was sorrow in the house, too. A heaviness all around. I asked Lyd if she'd noticed and she said, "It's *the grief*. It's probably because Grandfather Meagher died in this house. Mother loved her father, didn't she?" There was one framed photograph of Grandfather Meagher that hung on the dining-room wall. No matter where we moved in the room, his eyes stared at us under heavy brows.

The next night there was no thought of anyone sleeping. Granny's fever had not broken. Mother insisted that the onions had never failed and, grimly, kept on. Granny was wet with perspiration and again we changed her linen. We were in a state between wakefulness and sleep; heavy fatigue had slipped over us all. The three of us dozed uncomfortably in armchairs we'd squeezed around the two narrow beds in the sickroom. My joints were stiff and aching. In the middle of the night Granny hauled herself to a sitting position, bolt upright, and shouted, "What's the news, good or bad?" The onion plasters peeled off her as she rose.

We were so startled and so fatigued Mother and Lyd and I looked at one another and began to laugh — huge guffawing laughs — until tears rolled down our cheeks. Mother laughed the loudest. Granny Tracks held her tongue while she watched the three of us and then said disgustedly, "Damned fools," which set us off again. She lowered herself onto the sheet and dropped into a deep and prolonged sleep. The next day she began to get better. She refused to talk about her illness; it was as if it hadn't been.

I'd begun to get used to the trains next to Granny's. It was comforting to lie there and listen as they pulled out of Darley, their thin mournful wails trailing through the night. What I did not like was the sound of footsteps crossing the veranda when someone passed by outside in the dark. Lyd and I lay in the double bed staring at the ceiling. Heavy footsteps walked across the room. Our room, the front bedroom, was directly over the street.

"This place is starting to give me the creeps," Lyd said.

I tried to will myself to sleep. Footsteps crossed the room again. I felt Lyd's body tense beside me. Moments later — it seemed like moments later — I opened my eyes.

Lyd was sitting up staring at what I now saw at the foot of the bed. A greenish glow surrounded the figure of a man I did not know. He seemed edgeless, somehow, but no part of him moved. His eyes glowered from under heavy brows. Though he hadn't spoken, I knew he wanted us out of Granny's bed. He wanted Granny back in her own room.

I heard my voice give up a shout. The green glow faded and he was gone. Lyd ran to the light switch and turned it on. It was ten past four in the morning. We'd been asleep for hours. My heart was beating so quickly, my mouth so dry, I wasn't able to speak.

"We have to get out of Granny's bed," Lyd said.

We didn't talk about how we both knew this. Maybe, I told myself, maybe we shared the same bad dream. I tried to push the dream out of my mind. But there was something else, something about the heavy brows, that I couldn't forget. We didn't want to stay in the room any longer so we dragged the blankets down the tower stairs and spent the hours until daybreak huddled together on the couch.

Lorne was at the curb, in the Ford, waiting for us before breakfast. He'd brought Granny Tracks some tea from legumes he'd grown himself. He'd roasted the leaves and pods on cookie sheets in the farm-oven and packed them into a biscuit tin. Mother tried to persuade him to have eggs and bacon with us but he refused. He handed over the tea and stared at a patch in the linoleum.

Mother took advantage of Lorne's unannounced visit to send Lyd and me back to the farm. She was going to stay until Granny could manage the stairs and, after that, Aunt Arra would take over.

"Tell your father I'll get to the farm when I can," she said. "You two help Aunt Lucy with the meals, and keep an eye on Eddie." I knew she would stay until she was no longer needed. But when I looked at the dark shadows around her eyes, I knew she had fallen into the heaviness of that house and would have no chance to escape, or to get away.

Lyd and I gathered our clothes and changed the sheets and helped Granny back to her own big room. Sitting in bed in a knitted shrug, drinking Lorne's tea, she didn't look at all like delirious Granny Tracks smothered under onion plasters. Lorne would not come upstairs but Granny sent him a message. "If a person can get over the dog, he can get over the tail," she said. Lorne nodded at this when we went down and told him. I guess Granny Tracks had decided she wasn't finished with living after all.

Lyd sat by the window; I was in the middle between her and Lorne. I was watching Lorne's hands and feet because I half expected him to stop the car and start swearing. I was afraid he'd order me to take the wheel and drive through town. I didn't want to drive but I needn't have worried. Once we were out of town and on the Fifth Line, Lorne turned to Lyd and said, "The spider weaves its own web without the help of passers-by." He did not say this unkindly and I was afraid that Lyd would demand, "What, Lorne, what! For Cripes' sake, say what you mean."

But she did not. She stared out her window, and I stared straight ahead. Lorne had nothing to say to me. No grudge and no unfinished business. He drove along the gravel road, and calm descended beneath the blanket of his silence.

I began to wish that we would never get to the farm; that we could suspend ourselves between the homes of our separate grandparents and go on driving like this without ever stopping. Squeezed as I was between Lorne and Lyd, I felt the warming sun through the windshield and I smelled country: the scent of drying hay, cow manure, the mixture of weeds and crops and long grasses drifting through the open window. I pressed my back into the seat and closed my eyes.

I began to think of our river at home in Quebec; the way I walked to the cliff and stood looking down over rapids. I thought about how I sometimes chose one spot on a single wave and how I tried to hold that spot. No matter how hard I tried or how many times, my eyes shifted in the direction of current. Against my will, beyond my will, I could not focus on that single spot. I couldn't stop the perpetual motion, not for a fragment of a second. I knew that despite all of this, as soon as we left Darley and returned home, I'd go back and stand on that cliff and I'd try once more to seize the imaginary spot. To slow it down, even if it were only long enough for me to believe that this might be possible.

BOLERO

1955

The following spring, after break-up, the logs came down, the river dark with timber. Lyd and I went to bed on a Friday night and when we awoke the next morning there was a hush over the river, logs coming and coming in that steady inevitable flow. After breakfast I followed the shore away from the house and up towards higher ground. I stood on the cliff watching. The river narrowed at the beginning of the rapids and the mass dipped like a broad dark raft heading into fast water, whitecaps tossing the logs singly into the air and then catching and concealing them again.

As always, strays drifted to shore in front of the house. Most logs were round and smooth and stamped with the company brand but some still had bark attached, reminding that these were trees after all. We left the strays to sit in the sun and later went back to peel and crack the bark. During the following weeks, right into early summer, we collected insects with latticed wings folded flat the lengths of their backs, and used them as bait for bass.

The place we fished bass was below the rapids. Past morning glory and blunt-petalled wild rose. Past the cliff and the long meandering ruins of the old hydro wall, the crumbling prop that hemmed the point of land where the river curved at the fiercest part of the rapids. The first day we'd moved to Quebec, Father had taken us to see the wall. "Someone had the vision and imagination to harness this energy," he said. "But that was last century, not this. And I'm going to tell you right now. Don't lean on the wall, because it's old and cracked and someone's going to go with it."

Nothing could keep us away. We climbed the wall, straddled it, dug at it, pushed it, and when the water was not too high, walked it. We also feared it.

After the wall, the river calmed again and booms were strung out, chained end to end. We were not fooled by the calm. *Down below* was a bottomless place with tough roots twining through mud. Where weeds and bushes snared logs and where bodies drifted after they'd been tossed through rapids. Our paperboy had drowned in these rapids. Two winters ago, one of the girls who lived in the rooms behind Le Loup's store had also drowned. Both bodies had been found down below, stuffed under the booms.

It was Lyd who'd spied the hooks on a rainy day when we were taking turns with our friends climbing the ladder rungs and jumping from the attic platform to the barn floor below.

It was shortly after we'd moved — after Father had bought the house from Duffy. Lyd had found the hooks buried in dust behind an old storm door. Bulging pieces of iron with three great curves attached to a braided rope.

"Bodies!" Lyd was the one who dared the rest of us to do what she would not do herself but she commanded our attention because she was the eldest. I had just jumped to the boards and my leg-bones were wobbling from the impact. I climbed back up and heard her drop into her scaring voice. "Grappling hooks for bodies," she said quickly. "Bodies all stiff and water-bloated. The men drag the bottom to hook a shoulder or a leg. They lower the hooks from rowboats and make a huge splash." Her arms dropped iron through a black surface of river we all knew and imagined. "One man rows, two at the end of the boat drag."

How did she know this? Father hadn't told her because, later, he refused to talk about the hooks when we asked. But he set his mouth grimly and went with the men when they came to the back door after break-up, in the spring. It turned out that everyone in St. Pierre knew that the village grappling hooks were kept in Duffy's old barn.

After that, one of our summer games while swimming in the river with our friends became "Dead Body." Someone would dip beneath the surface and remember. Would rise with cheeks puffed and shriek, "Dead body below! Dead body!" Our legs ran thickly through water and we scraped knees and feet in the race for shore. Each of us had seen the bloated features of the waterlogged, had felt the hand of the drowned tighten around an ankle; each of us knew that wherever we might place a foot we would step on a body with swollen sealed eyes.

In fact, we never swam down below, by the booms. Our only swimming was in the cove in front of the house, shallow and quiet with its own current but safely above the rapids. It was where we had learned to dog-paddle. It was where Mother viewed the river as a danger that could sweep away her children's limp rag bodies into its current. She had never learned to swim and sat on shore on a towel, wearing shorts, a blouse buttoned down the front, the tails of it tied in a knot at her waist. She stayed there, sunning her legs, crooking a finger at us when we waded out too far. Standing up and hollering when we pretended not to see.

It was the first week of July and our parents announced that they were having a corn roast. Not at the usual site on broad shale in front of the house but following the bank up onto the high flat part of the cliff where there were twelve white pines, grown tall and full with their bundles of soft needles. Quite naturally, we'd always called the place the Pines. It was halfway to the wall. Below the cliff were the first whitecaps, the place where true fast water began. The river was still high from spring run-off but the change of current could be seen from this very spot.

Eddie had left for Ontario as soon as school was out, and was now at Grampa King's farm. Lyd and I had been helping Father and Duffy and Roy, from the club, collect driftwood and the smallest stray logs along shore. We pretended to find logs that were not branded, and dragged them onto the rocks to dry.

The men did not have their own club; it was the second annual party of the sewing club of their wives — and Rebecque, Duffy's girlfriend. It was the summer the women made cotton sundresses with bolero tops that came halfway down their backs, with close-fitting sleeves ending just above the elbow. *Clever cover-ups with a classic look* was printed on the pattern.

Recently, on a scorching day, Roy's wife, Mona, of the little feet, had been shopping in Hull when a policeman approached and advised her that she must put on her jacket. She was carrying her new cotton bolero over her arm. Her shoulders should not be bare, said the policeman, even though he could see that the sundress was held up by a two-inch width of straps. She could be fined fifty dollars or spend a month in jail.

The women of the club were buzzing with this story.

"Maudit fou," Rebecque said, of the policeman *and* the law, which was suspect. When she spoke, this came out sounding like *"Moodzee foo."* No one knew if a Quebec ban on bare shoulders really existed. But the enforcement of it came out of the same morality that prevented Lyd and me from wearing our shorts on rue Principale in St. Pierre. Even to run up to Le Loup's for a pound of sliced bologna we had to change into a skirt. We could wear shorts in our yard and in the fields but if we were seen on the main street of the village, the priest would send us home.

Mother's sundress, made from the same pattern used by the other women, was linen, not cotton. The colour of deep summer sky embedded with a myriad of tiny yellow stars. You had to stand close to the material to see the stars, they were so minute. When the last stitches were done, Mother pushed the iron over the new dress, back-forth, back-forth, flattening the straps last. The bolero, not meant to join in front, curved perfectly over her bust. The first time she wore the dress was to buy groceries in Hull. Warned by Mona, she kept the bolero on. Before she left to catch the bus she stood at the long mirror that had once belonged to Duffy's runaway wife. She turned to view all angles of herself and patted her hips. She wanted her dress to be slightly different, and had added false pleats at the waist. It was hard to tell if she was pleased with it or not. She arched one arm and then the other over her head to check the sleeves. She pulled at a thread and then muttered to herself and left to cross the field so that she could catch the bus to town.

Rebecque sometimes came over to exercise with Mother in our house after supper. They pushed the kitchen table against the wall and twirled the radio dial till they found music they liked. They sat on the floor, one at each end of the linoleum. Legs outstretched, arms outstretched, palms down, fingertips leading, they crossed the room on their bottoms, shifting forward first one buttock, then the other. When they passed, each collapsed an elbow and pulled an imaginary cord. "Toot-toot!" they shouted, trying to keep the beat of "Ragmop" or "Slow Poke" or "Gonna Get Along Without Ya Now."

Lyd and I refused to watch this display and sat outside on the steps until they were finished. We stayed close enough to hear what they were saying, but we were mortified by their behaviour. Mother and Rebecque laughed at us. "We are firming our buttocks," they said deliberately. "Just you wait until you're our age, just you wait."

All day Saturday, party food had been arriving. A copper boiler appeared. Duffy carried in a sack filled with corn, and he and Rebecque went down to the river to husk. Duffy laughed like Gildersleeve. He told us he'd driven through field roads the night before, to steal the corn, and we half believed him. Lyd and I followed him and Rebecque to the river and offered to help because we liked to be near them. Rebecque was forever teasing about kissing him through his moustache. By now they were living together in Rebecque's house in the village but they were not like our parents or the other couples in the club. *They were not married.* They were *living in sin,* but they were in love.

Father organized a work party to arrange a circle of stones back from the edge of the cliff and we began to lug wood. We'd been collecting all week but he wouldn't let us take it to the site until the last minute in case it was stolen. The cliff could not be seen from the house. It was the first time a party would be held there and I could not see the point of it. Every fork, every stick of wood, every cob of corn and slab of butter had to be carried. It wasn't like ducking in and out of the house when ice was needed, or when someone had to use the bathroom.

How would Lyd and I know what was going on?

Would they dance under the twelve pines? How would they get music up there? It wouldn't be pieces like "Coppelia Waltz," played on our record player in the living room while Mother, holding our backs stiff, twirled us, one-two-three, one-two-three. It wouldn't be "Dizzy Fingers" on piano. It would be radio songs: "Secret Love," "Pretty Baby," "Walkin' My Baby Back Home."

It was the music that made Lyd and me decide to sneak to the party after dark. We'd hide in the bushes and watch them dance. We'd go the long way round, skirt the Pines by taking a lower path to the booms and come back towards the party from down below. We knew every bush that would conceal us and we'd be able to see by the light of the fire. The adults would be drinking, the men beer, the women gin and tonic, and we'd be able to watch them misbehave.

The club women had decided to wear slacks, Mother announced, and she pressed her own with a damp cloth during the lull between late afternoon and early evening. Duffy and Rebecque had gone home to change; the fresh corn was piled into three brown shopping bags, ready to be boiled. Father kept changing his mind about the beer. Should he take washtubs and hack at a block of ice to keep the bottles cold? Should he carry up river water and stand the beer in that?

Mother wore a short-sleeved nylon sweater to match her beige slacks. She applied lipstick, and then a spot of rouge on each cheek, rubbed with her finger upward and outward over the bone. She had the Spanish look, again, I thought. This time her long hair was fastened at the back and flowed down over her shoulders. With her face turned away from us she looked like mystery. I remembered the name book Mimi and I had looked in, the day we'd buried the rosary. *Moor,* I said to myself. *Dark One.*

Mother turned to Lyd and me and looked like her ordinary self again. "I don't know if I'll be warm enough when the breeze comes up off the river," she said. "What do you think?" She turned again, towards the mirror.

As if the three of us had planned the moment together, she went back to the door of her closet and removed her bolero from the sundress on its hanger. She slipped the bolero over her sweater. The tiny stars seemed to multiply, to pull inward.

She surveyed herself in the long mirror, once again, and said, "Do you think I look nice? What do you think?"

Father had come into the room and we watched as he turned his head to look at her. I thought he might go over to her; I thought he might touch her. But he didn't.

Anyway, I knew she wasn't really asking.

Lyd and I made cheese-and-mustard sandwiches and bided our time. We watched the clock and watched the clock and finally set out through the back screen door and got our feet onto a path that was so black it almost disappeared. I thought I knew every root and anthill but I kept stumbling. What I hadn't allowed for was the roar. Usually I never heard the rapids because they were always there; now they pounded like drums rolling in thunder. It occurred to me that I'd never been deep into the Pines at night. Lyd was starting to change her mind. We took turns hanging on to each other's sleeve.

"Did you know it would be so dark?" she said.

"We're not quitting. We made up our minds."

"Yeah, well if Father catches us, he'll be madder than hops."

"Too bad." I got in front and yanked my arm free. "Whether you go back or not, I'm still going." I knew she'd rather be at home.

"Jesus," Lyd muttered. "Jesus Cripes." But I could hear her footsteps behind me.

We'd made a wide semicircle and approached the Pines from below as planned. A ridge of the old wall leaned out over the rapids in a meandering curve and gave us a landmark to follow. The bushes opened up and the path widened. From here we could see sparks shooting up from the fire and we heard deep distant laughter.

"Duffy," Lyd said. "I hear the moustache."

She couldn't return now because it was darker behind than in front. I was glad, because I didn't want to be there alone. We left the path and stuck to a thickness of trees far back from the open cliff. The entire club was there in silhouette, circled round a crackling fire. There was Father holding a bottle of beer; Mona, her husband, Roy, hovering as if he had to be right there to protect her little feet; Rebecque in wonderful tight red party strides, close-dancing with Duffy, who kept kissing her neck.

"It's the perfume," I said. "Where she puts it. Right on the pulse."

"Ici! Ici!" Lyd said, jabbing her finger, and we doubled over, loving Rebecque.

We crouched down to settle in. The men were going back and forth to the washtubs for beer, the women dancing with one another's husbands — except for Duffy and Rebecque. A log was kicked into the fire from one side and burst out the other. The laughter was shrill, edged with foolishness.

"They're worse than we are," I told Lyd, but that was okay. We knew who they were; we'd been eavesdropping on them for years. We just wanted to be there to make sure we knew what they were up to and that what they were up to was the same old thing.

Now the radio was playing "Jambalaya." Everyone stopped and pointed glasses and bottles up into the air. They planted their feet and became a chorus over the rapids. They could not be said to be in harmony.

"They're half snapped already," Lyd said.

"Not Mom," I said. "Look."

She did have a drink in her hand and we knew it was gin and tonic but she wasn't holding it in the air and she wasn't singing, either. She knew every showtune, every line from every musical, every radio song. But she didn't shout her songs into the sky. Our mother sang privately, to herself and to her children. She'd been doing it since we were born and probably before that, too. In the kitchen, a tea towel wrapped around her waist because she couldn't be bothered tying an apron. Our mother, her dark hair floating over her shoulders, her bolero drenched with stars.

Now, she set her drink on boards that had been propped on two logs, and looked through the circle of fire. She was by herself, away from the others who were singing, and she reached down into the paper shopping bag and started dropping corn, one cob, another, and another, into the boiler. She did this methodically, as if she were thinking about something else. And then she straightened, and looked through the fire again. I thought I saw her lips move but I wasn't close enough to figure out what she was saying.

The members of the chorus, shouting to the treetops, arms around one another's waists, were finding themselves very funny.

"What the hell!" It was Roy. He had his fly open and a dark stream had already arced into the bushes beside us. He turned his back one direction and Lyd and I twisted in the other.

"You little buggers," he said. "Get the hell home before I tell your father." He was fumbling with his pants. We thought he'd shout for Father right there and then.

"How did you get up here?" He hissed at us, his fly finally done up.

"We came the long way," I said. "From down below. Are you going to tell?"

"You bet I'll tell. Now get the hell out of here. Go back the same way you came."

We bolted along the line of bushes, into a night as black as the waves, heading for the wall so we could follow its curve to the path. Lyd was in front this time and I was shouting.

"Where the hell did he come from? I thought they were all singing. Goddam him sneaking up like that. He almost peed all over us."

We reached the wall and leaned against it. "Mother was saying something," I told Lyd. "I was trying to see what she was saying." I started shoving against the wall as hard as I could.

"Are you crazy?" Lyd said. "The wall's going to fall."

"You're the one who's crazy," I said. "The wall's a foot and a half thick. It'll never fall."

I kicked at it again, and shoved some more. But I gave up and we walked slowly home along the path, hearing the party behind us, never considering the hands groping up out of the black water as we skirted the booms, down below.

"Did you see Roy's penis?" I said.

"No, did you?"

We started laughing hysterically, and ran the rest of the way, climbing in through our bedroom window, even though there was no need to with our parents up in the Pines. We laughed and laughed and laughed and got into our big double bed and didn't draw a line down the middle of the bottom sheet or fight or swear at each other or make threats that would have to be resolved or carried out the next day. We went to sleep thinking of Roy telling or not telling, of almost being peed on, of Rebecque dancing in her tight red pants, of music floating up through the pines. We slept right through the blackest hours of the night and didn't wake until we heard new sounds and crying and shouts in the dark. The barn door banging and the hooks thrown out of the attic to the earth below.

"What," Lyd said. "What." She got out of bed and I could see her long legs in the moonlight as she jumped from one foot to the other. We went through the summer kitchen and stood at the back screen. All the lights had been turned on in the house. Rebecque walked in and pulled us both tightly against her chest.

"What," Lyd kept saying. "What. Tell us what. Please, Rebecque, please tell us."

Because we still didn't know. Because we'd been sound asleep when Mother walked to the edge of the cliff, slept while her left foot tripped and crossed over her right, slept while she lost her balance and slipped silent over the edge, disappearing in full firelight view of her husband and her closest friends. Looking into Rebecque's face we still did not know. And it would be some time before we would be able to imagine the weightlessness, the air rushing past the two spots of rouge on her cheeks, her head bobbing in the white-tipped waves, the breeze resting, now, in her long dark hair.

PLAY PIANO

1955

Mother was in every shadow of the house. In the furniture that had moved with us from Darley and in what was left of the furniture abandoned by Duffy. She was under the wine-coloured carpet that Lyd beat with the broom and inside the smoker with spool legs, and on the wicker settee in the porch. I thought of her, too, when I picked away at the keys or pounded chords on our old Heintzman piano. At night I dreamed the weight of it pressing through the floor, going down like a mahogany ship through waves of hardwood, sinking to the crawl space below. I dreamed unthinkables — worms, moles, voles, weasels, proofs of which I hoped never to see. I dreamed Mother trapped below, trying to reach up to get to us, and I awoke, terrified, in the dark.

Sometimes she stood in the doorway beside the long mirror

that had belonged to Duffy's runaway wife. From the piano bench I could see the front of her but in the mirror there was no image of her back. With two fingers I picked out a melody she used to sing: "Norah, the Pride of Kildare." But when I played — softly, so the others wouldn't hear — I substituted Mother's name. "Maura, sweet Maura," I sang. "What mortal could injure a blossom so rare."

Mimi's Tante Florence had taught me how to chord and move my hands over the length of the keyboard, switching octaves. At home, Father stood behind me, hands resting on my shoulders, and said to anyone who might be visiting — there were people in the house constantly now — "She's a natural. Listen to my child-between. She's an absolute natural." I knew without turning around that his eyes were filling, and I tried to squirm away.

When no one was around, I wedged my way *behind* the piano. It was beached kitty-corner at the end of the living room and had been left like that all the years since its abandonment by Duffy. "Too heavy to move," Father said. "The floor can't take the weight of it, shifting around."

The back of the piano, unlike the deep rich stain of the front, was uncamouflaged — raw pale wood. I stood there, silent, scarcely breathing. It was like being inside an after-image; holding a negative to the light, seeing mouth and eye sockets white and exposed beyond skin.

"He'd steal the coppers off a deadman's eyes," Father snapped as he crossed the room, and I realized with a shock that he didn't know I was there. He stood for a moment in the doorway of the porch and said, "That puts the kibosh on *that*."

There were other days when he recited mournful snippets of Tennyson that lined up inside his head.

. . . my whole soul grieves,
    At the moist rich smell of the rotting leaves

He wandered sorrowfully from room to room and I could hardly bear to look at him. I heard him, though, from behind the piano.

I heard Eddie, too, when he ran through the living room and yelled, mysteriously, "I hate you!" And Lyd went banging through the house, from room to room, looking for me. "I can't find her!" she shouted back to Father. "I know she's hiding so she won't have to do the dishes!" Under her breath she said, "Damn her." And then she added, "Jesus Poêle," a curse we'd recently admitted to our vocabulary.

Implicitly, from my piano bench in front, and from the triangle of space behind, I knew that the piano had begun to belong to me. Father seemed to know this, too, because he announced one day that he'd sent for a home-study course all the way from Dallas, Texas. I checked the atlas when he held up the ad from the *Star Weekly*. *Play Piano*, said the ad. *Easy Home Lessons.*

"Who wants to learn?" Father said. "Properly."

Lyd was not interested. Nor was Eddie. I was elected. I even volunteered. Well, I thought. I'll come out from behind and take my place on the long bench and I will learn what real pianists know. Lyd and I argued over what I would be called — "Pee-ANN-ist," or "PEE-a-nist," which sounded too much like penis, to me.

While waiting for Dallas, Texas, I began to explore the piano as if I'd never seen it before. The mahogany bench was stuffed with old sheet music and I kneeled on the floor, propped the lid and shuffled through stacks of classical works, and songs popular at the turn of the century. I asked Duffy about these but he was surprised that they were there. "Maybe it was the mother of my runaway wife. Or the grandmother," he said, when I showed him a signature written on a cover.

What fascinated me were the ribbons of black beads rising and falling across the page. This was the code I had to break. I began in earnest to limber my fingers against any flat surface I passed, even layers of shale when I sat on the banks of the river in front of our home.

In my sleep, Mother smiled as I chorded. But it was in my sleep, too, that I saw her in the river, a place she'd never been until her death except to wade up to her ankles while Eddie splashed around, or while she'd helped Lyd and me wash our hair. The dreams always ended the same way. Mother in the waves. Me waking and sitting upright, chills running through my body. I said to myself each time: *When I went to bed, she was here. When I woke up, she was gone.* It had happened that quickly. It was the difference between *this* and *that*.

The old Heintzman had columnar legs and a hinged top. Its front panel was the size of a small door, which I could raise and rest on top of my head. This was like lifting a stage curtain and in one fell swoop, as Father said, catching the actors and prompters off guard. I plucked at the hammers, all maple in colour and padded with green felt, and they plinked in a muted way as if somehow their musical journey had been incomplete. Even with the weight bearing down on my head, I never tired of being a voyeur to the Gepetto-like workshop inside my piano. I ran fingernails over taut wires — short and thin for high notes, tight thick coils for low. I pressed the ivory keys and guessed at corresponding gaps as the hammers fell forward. When I reached for the foot pedals, the entire keyboard rose and fell like big-bosomed breathing. To clean the keys I used a cloth dipped in a cereal bowl of warm milk carried, with careful ceremony, from the kitchen. It was Father who'd heard about the milk — he'd put out the word in the hotel one Friday night. I rubbed its whiteness into the keys until stickiness and smudges disappeared, and when I was satisfied, I tugged the lid and closed its clever concealing curve over the keyboard of my piano.

Back I went to the river, trying to sing, trying to practise songs I'd been picking out with one hand. My fingers tapped accompaniment on shale:

> *En roulant ma boule roulant,*
> *En roulant ma boule.*

Mrs. Perry had taught this to us during the last days of June when we'd been impatient to get out of school. We'd been cooped up, all the grades in one room, moist waves of early summer heat wafting through the screenless windows. Mrs. Perry knew we were fed up. She had taught us "Riding on a Donkey," too, and we'd raced about the school yard shouting:

Were you ever in Quebec,
Stowing timber on a deck
Where there's a king with a golden crown
Riding on a donkey?

Our new school was supposed to be ready in the fall; it was even rumoured that for every two grades, there would be a new teacher. At one time this had mattered. Now, I didn't care if I ever went back to school.

When the course materials arrived from Dallas, Texas, Father was right there to unpack the contents. Lyd was there, too, but she would not look me in the eye. I knew she didn't want anything to do with the lessons, especially as it meant reporting to Father. A stutter of doubt blipped through me along with what I suddenly saw as an extra burden, an invisible life-burden stuck to the contents of this box.

The name of company and course was *Play Piano, Eighty Easy Lessons,* and the lessons were divided into ten folders. Two sheets of paper had been inserted under the cover of Lesson One. The first was to say that a place would be held for Trude King — there was my name in print — in the Music Hall of Fame. I imagined some Dallas, Texas, musical space and thought of my triangle behind the piano, its dust rolls and its raw wood.

The second was a testimonial:

Dear Director:

For a long time our unfortunate daughter, Clara, has been a problem. My wife and I asked ourselves many times if we had done something wrong. She had no interests; she had no friends; she received poor grades in school. I am not exaggerating when I say we were more than a little worried. We managed to locate and buy an old piano, and hired a blind man to tune it. Then, we sent for *Play Piano*. At first, Clara reacted the way she always did, without interest. But her attitude changed the moment she dug into the box. Now, she plays like a natural.

I suppose you've already guessed what I'm going to say next. Clara can sit at the keyboard and play "Beautiful, Beautiful Brown Eyes" until it would break your heart. At school, her teachers are rubbing their eyes. Believe me, I'm going to tell everyone I know about *Play Piano*. Our daughter is on Lesson Seventeen and going strong. *Play Piano* has changed her life.

Faithfully yours,
Mr. X.

A part of me hunkered down. I would ignore Lyd. It was not so easy to ignore Father, his face releasing hope. Somewhere, I told myself, Clara is teaching herself *Eighty Easy Lessons* on an old piano tuned by a blind man. This very moment she might be running through "Beautiful, Beautiful Brown Eyes," for old time's sake. As I thought about her, I knew one thing for certain. Just as surely as Clara had escaped her fate, I was being drawn into mine.

When the others left me alone, I began to inspect the folders. Alternating with the text were pictures of couples or party-goers grouped about a piano. Never an upright like ours, but a baby grand with a propped lid. *Baby grand,* I whispered, loving the sound. *Baby grand.*

The women in the pictures looked sideways to the camera. They wore floral-patterned dresses and dark lipstick and had page-boy hair. Mother had worn her hair like that for a time, but mostly she'd pinned it in a vertical roll, for the Spanish look. Two weeks after Mother's funeral, Rebecque had come to the house on a Sunday after we'd come home from Hull where we'd been to church. Father had asked her to help sort out Mother's clothes. Duffy took Father and Eddie to the end of the backyard, where we had a horseshoe pit, and the clang of horseshoes against the iron peg paused and rang through the screens while Rebecque began to go through Mother's closet and dresser drawers.

Lyd and I sat glumly on Mother's side of the bed. We were supposed to tell Rebecque what we wanted to keep, what we wanted out of the way. The jewellery, we divided into two small heaps on the bedspread. There were a few sweaters we could wear, a cardigan, a short coat for Lyd. We did not look at the party dresses in the plastic wardrobes, and told Rebecque we'd decide on those another day. We did not want the rest. But at the last moment, through Rebecque's tact and kindness, I made a leap for two of Mother's long-sleeved blouses — a rayon and a silk — just as Rebecque was folding them and placing them in the bag.

"Those are too old," Lyd said. "Way too old for you."

She was right. One was a soft pale pink; the other, a sheer off-white. When Mother had worn them, her slip and bra straps had shown through. But I didn't want them for wearing. I gave no explanation, and neither Lyd nor Rebecque argued.

Later, I hung them at the end of our own long closet. I put them beside the stones of the chimney where they would always be warm. When I was alone, I walked into the closet and stood between the blouses, my face pressed against them. I believed that I could smell my mother. The scent of her, her bits of rouge, her perfume, even a hint of deodorant were in those blouses and I stood there, drawing her in, through the dark.

As I continued to look through the folders from *Play Piano,* I read other letters printed at the beginnings of lessons as if to spur me on. These were from both men *and* women. The men played as a hobby or to entertain friends after trying days at the office or when they relaxed after being on the road. One woman planned to become a concert pianist after she finished being a housewife. All of them swore that *Play Piano* had changed their lives.

At the bottom of the box I found a long black-and-white chart to slide in behind the keys. Each lettered key showed me how to tell one note from another. Lesson One promised that before I could say "Jack Robinson," I would no longer have to rely on this chart, which was only a prop to get me started.

The chart had to be centred at middle C, and from the beginning I sensed this to be the most important key on my piano. It was my favourite; in C I recognized a core, a touchstone for all musicians, a lighthouse that beckoned, when we floundered offshore. All other keys existed only as they related to middle C.

I spent days and weeks filling in exercise sheets, shading notes, whipping through the first eight lessons so I could move on to folder number two. I stowed the chart-prop in the bench and never looked at it again. I tackled "Sweet Betsy from Pike" and learned the words to all the verses. I began to skip whole pages that did not interest me.

What *did* interest me was reading about the people who'd studied before. *Last night, I attended a concert,* a woman wrote, *and I was careful to watch the posture of the pianist. He knew how to stay alert but relaxed at the keyboard.*

I had never been to a concert except for the Christmas concerts at Stone, my one-room school. I sat at the piano and thought of the words *alert but relaxed.* I flung out my arms and tried to let go. I was to think clearly about my problems — this was the message I read in Lesson Nine.

I knew my problems. One of them was that I'd given up on counting. I'd made some attempt to learn whole notes, quarters, sixteenths (a sixteenth is no longer than a grunt, I read), but counting did not interest me and I made up my mind to play everything by ear. This meant I had to find other ways to learn melody. Knowing nothing of my decision, Father tried to boost my attempts to learn. On weekends, he stood behind me, his hands resting heavily on my shoulders. "Keep playing," he said. "Don't stop, even if you make a mistake. Keep up the beat! Keep up the beat!" One Saturday, he took the bus to Hull and crossed the river to Ottawa and went to Orme's on Sparks Street. He came home with sheet music for "The Whiffenpoof Song," and a march and two-step, "The Midnight Fire Alarm."

"The Whiffenpoof" was so complicated I could only bang out the top notes of the right hand. Father stood behind, filling in with "Baas" when I couldn't go on. "The Midnight Fire Alarm" had no words, so with this we had to take our chances. Father stomped his feet in marching order behind my back. *"Keep up the beat!"* He clapped his hands and drummed on the mahogany and it took two weekends to get past the first twelve bars. After one of our Saturday afternoon sessions, Eddie said, as if he were trying to spare me, "Your playing stinks, you know." But he said it with pity because he and I knew that in our family we never gave up.

We had been checking the progress of the new school all summer and twice Lyd and I had walked the mile and a half to watch its angles and contours take shape. It was in a kind of no man's land between village and country, hunkered in the middle of a long field. We would still have to take the orange bus, but now every Protestant child for miles around — village and country — would be brought to this place. We would study here until grade eight. After that, we would be transferred to the high school, in Hull.

Lyd and I were worried. Living beside the river as we did, we rarely saw our classmates during the summer. When it was time to go back to school we did not want anyone feeling sorry for us.

Workmen at the site warned us to stay away from the earth pit of the gym and auditorium, so we peered in along the front of the school through taped windows, and guessed which rooms would be ours. We'd heard that the grade eights would not have to share space and Lyd was certain that she'd be in the first room down the hall from the office.

Eventually, an announcement arrived in the mail to say that teachers had been hired and classrooms were finished. Inside work on the gym would not be complete until November. The date had been set in that month for an opening ceremony.

I continued to practise at my piano. On Saturdays, Father was behind me, hands pressing down on my shoulders. I was skipping from one folder to another now, relying less and less on any ability to read notes and more and more on my own ear. At night, in my sleep, Mother looked on from the doorway by the mirror, while I pumped the pedals and pounded the keys.

It had been weeks since Lyd and I had spoken of Mother, though words sometimes flew out of our mouths:

You're supposed to soak that for ten minutes to get the dirt out.

How do you know?

Mom said.

You're not supposed to drink tea before bed. It keeps you awake.

Who said?

Mom.

Then we walked away to separate parts of the house, each avoiding the other's face because it looked like one's own — stricken.

At the end of summer, everything speeded up. My birthday came and went and I invited Mimi for supper. After we'd eaten the cake, I went to the river and cried.

"Don't worry," Mimi said. "It isn't true that if you cry on your birthday, you cry all year." She added, soberly, "It was like this when my father died, I remember. Come to my place and we'll laugh," she said. "You can practise French with Grand-mère. You can put your fingers around her little wrist."

But I went back to my own house and stood in the closet, the blouses brushing my face in the dark.

In September we walked through the doors of our new school and I learned that I had not one but two new teachers, though the second was only temporary. My classroom teacher was Mr. Crawley — the first male teacher I'd ever met. He had a flabby face and a big behind and hair the colour of sand. He constantly took us by surprise because of his mood changes and I worried all the time I was in his class. He stalked us backwards between rows, his back to the blackboard, and tried to surprise us face to face. Very quickly, he earned the name Crawfish. What set me on edge was that no matter what I did to stay out of his way, he hovered around my desk. I would turn around and he'd be there; I'd step into the room and he'd be behind me, the hairs of a tiny moustache sprouting over his upper lip. I did not like looking at him because he had what Lyd and I called the sorrowful eye and he had picked me to fix it on.

My second teacher, but only on Friday afternoons, was Miss Tina. I never learned her last name. Miss Tina was as kind as Crawfish was unpredictable. At the beginning of the year, fourteen girls, aged twelve and thirteen, were rounded up and led to the unfinished gym through an outside door. Although the gym itself had not been completed, the stage at the end was ready for use. We walked across a row of planks and up a side flight of steps to reach its blond hardwood floor.

The reason the fourteen of us had been chosen was because, at the opening ceremony in November, we were to be part of the entertainment. We were told that we were going to learn a dance. To teach us, a real dance teacher had been found. The lessons were free. No one knew where Miss Tina had come from but she told us it was her job to convince us that we could coordinate our limbs.

We could hear sawing noises above the ceiling at the far end of the gym. During that first lesson, fourteen of us leaned into the wall of bricks and stared. Miss Tina was the first adult woman we'd ever seen who had no breasts. Not only did she have no breasts, she wore no bra. What she did wear was a skimpy black leotard that accentuated the flat board of her chest.

Tap tap tap, shuffle shuffle. Miss Tina darted, relaxed and let go. She called to us, "In out, in out, tap tap tap." So busy were her lower limbs she did not seem to notice that she had no breasts.

To my astonishment, my own feet, after an hour of awkward tries, began to shuffle in time with the feet of the other girls. Miss Tina opened a portable record player on stage and set and reset a record she'd brought with her while she coaxed us step by step. We would not be required to buy tap shoes, she explained, because that would mean unnecessary expense for our parents. "What we're learning are shuffle-taps," she said. "We just keep time to the music and point our toes."

The top-hat piece we were working on was "Pretty Baby." I knew the song because Mother used to sing it, but it was one I'd never tried to play at home on my piano. By the end of the lesson, we'd begun to like Miss Tina. And she actually liked us, we could tell.

We walked back across the planks as slowly as we could so we wouldn't have to return to our home rooms before taking the bus. Most of us in the dance group were in Crawfish's six-seven class. Lyd would be waiting for me outside the door of her room, the grade eights. We tried to stay together to ward off the pitying glances thrown our way by our classmates. We knew that tragedy had happened in our family but we wanted to be treated the same as everyone else. Mrs. Perry, who had the grade twos now in the new school, stopped me in the hall and, in front of everyone, hugged me close and said how sorry she was about my mother. In the lunchroom the same day, a grade eight girl named Gladys carried over half a sardine sandwich and put it on my lap. I had my own sandwich and hated the crunch of spines in sardines but I didn't know what else to do but eat it.

The most surprising thing of all was that we were expected to carry on. Make our lunches at night, go to school the next morning. Come home, do our homework. Go to bed and back to school in the morning again. I could not, though I tried, remember the last time Mother had touched me — to put her hand to my cheek, or to stand me in front of her knees while she sat and brushed my hair.

At the end of the third lesson, Miss Tina told our little dance troupe that we were beginning to perform like real dancers. We were able to swish along in an even line and seemed to be getting the hang of it. While she was packing up, three of us went over to the old piano that had been moved in from Brick and hoisted up to the new stage. We had ten minutes till bus time and began to take turns showing each other chords. When it was my turn, I played from memory "The Pride of Kildare." It was the song I sang to my mother silently when I believed she was standing by the mirror, and I knew the whole thing by heart.

Miss Tina, her body curved over the record player, straightened to listen. She asked me to play again and, on the spot, decided to reduce our dance line to thirteen so that I could play accompaniment. She went to her dance bag and pulled out the sheet music for "Pretty Baby."

"Take it home with you," she said. "Just try it out and see what happens. "You have a lovely touch on the keyboard."

I did not want attention drawn to myself but I could see that Miss Tina thought this an honour. My mind flashed to Dallas, Texas, and I panicked. Since school had started, I'd paid little attention to *Eighty Easy Lessons*. I explained to Miss Tina that I didn't know how to read sheet music — not properly. First, I would have to learn the piece by ear. Even then, it would be pretty skimpy.

"Then take the record home, too," she said. "See what you can do, and bring everything back to me next Friday."

I wanted to push it all back at her but I didn't know how. I began my descent from the stage and my shoe caught in a layer of cardboard that had been set down to protect the platform next to the stairs. I heard my voice shout, "Jesus Poêle," and I landed on the planks below, unhurt. I grabbed the record and the sheet music from the floor and looked up to stare straight into Miss Tina's absent chest. It was all I could do to keep from crying when she rushed down to help.

"Live music will add so much to the opening number," she said. She smiled at me. It was very hard not to like Miss Tina.

Somehow, somewhere, after I'd been forced to announce my coming performance, Father found a blind man to tune my piano. None of us had ever met a blind man, though Father had, lots of times, he said. He went into a long drawn-out story about when he was nineteen and walking on the road near the farm outside Darley. A man a hundred feet ahead of him was struck by a speeding car.

"The car came out of the night without warning," Father said. "He never knew what hit him. The sonofabitch behind the wheel didn't have the guts to stop. And the head — the poor bugger was decapitated — rolled right down the centre of the road."

"Was the man blind?" I asked, wondering at the connection.

"How the hell should I know? When I got to the head, its eyes were wide open. They were looking right through me."

So. My idea of what a blind person looked like was considerably distorted by the staring head rolling down the road.

Father usually took the bus to Hull Saturday mornings to order groceries that would be delivered the same afternoon. This day, he delayed the trip because the piano tuner was coming. Lyd and Eddie and I took up position on the front steps.

"When the blind man comes," said Father, as if he'd thought this through carefully, "I'm asking you not to stare." He looked weary and helpless, which surprised us and added weight to the blind man's visit. "Can't you go round to the backyard?" he said. But we would not be dislodged. Finally, he joined us on the steps, binoculars hanging from his neck.

A battered yellow convertible with the top down was sighted across the field. It was a sunny October day and the convertible turned at the river and approached along our dirt road. Eddie, awed by its arrival, was moved to stand on the grass.

There were two occupants: the blind man in a broad-shoul-dered three-piece suit, a bowler hat pressed to his forehead; and his wife, the driver. The blind man did not carry a white cane but looked jovial enough when his wife pushed him, with practised firm shoves, and got him stumbling up the steps and through the front door. We scattered to both sides of the porch as Father waved his hands behind the blind man's back and then we followed, hovering in the doorway between the dining room and living room.

Father spoke to the blind man and his wife as if they were hard of hearing but they nodded and smiled as if that were just fine. The blind man, a head taller than his wife, had a watch-chain that dipped across the front of his vest. Eddie and I looked at each other in disbelief: how did he tell time?

Inside the house the bowler hat came off and was placed on the back of the chesterfield. The blind man's wife rolled up her sleeves and pushed her husband towards the piano. Before they got down to business he turned to the place each of us was standing and said in a low rumble, "Howarya." He then proceeded, board by board, to take my piano apart. Even the lid to the keyboard lifted off, and at this, his wife cried out as if she couldn't help herself, "Oh darling, if you could only see these ivories." She was an experienced assistant, for she stayed and helped prop the boards and opened the black toolcase so he could get started on the inside work. Then she left him and went outside to sit with Father on the front steps so she could watch the view.

Lyd and Eddie and I made an excessively loud departure for the piano tuner's benefit, and escaped through the back door. We looked at one another. The real blind man could not compete with the head rolling down the road, the eyes that for all time had penetrated Father. None of us had had a close look at his eyes. Lyd had expected him to be wearing dark glasses. Eddie thought the eyeballs were loose, rolling around and hitting the inside of his head.

"He's probably fake," I said. "He can probably see."

"Then why would he let his wife push him around?" said Lyd, and we couldn't answer that.

"Oh, for Cripes' sake," Lyd said, "he's only blind." She left and went around the side of the house, heading for the front. I decided to tiptoe back inside and when I reached the entrance to the living room I could see Lyd and Eddie staring in through the window.

I had paused in front of Duffy's full-length mirror and now I stood watching the blind man's fingers as they moved rapidly in and around pegs and hammers, fastening ribbonlike strips to wire hooks. Every few minutes his large hands came down heavily on the keys, *bang bang*.

I stood like that for a long time. The longer I stood the more I was afraid to move because the blind man would hear me and think I'd been spying. My legs began to cramp. I could see Lyd through the window, beckoning me to come out, but I might as well have been frozen in Statue Tag. I stared at my own unhappy face, my pins-and-needles body, in the mirror. Just as I was about to bolt, two blind eyes rolled in my direction and the mouth said, "You can't be comfortable all cramped like that."

This both shocked and freed me and I mumbled, "I'm all right." I crossed the room quickly and walked deliberately past him, letting him know that I'd watch whomever I liked in my own house. I sat on the front steps and his wife squinted at me and patted my shoulder. "Poor motherless child," she said, and I was furious that she felt sorry for me. She didn't seem to notice, and called back cheerily through the screen, "Almost done, darling?"

His hands answered *bang bang* on one low key. He'd been turning his head this way and that before I left the room and

I wondered if he'd been trapping sound waves so he wouldn't be fooled and tighten something that would leave a sour note on my piano. I squirmed on the front steps until Father, who looked as uncomfortable as I'd ever seen him, gave me his warning look.

"What a view," said the blind man's wife, looking out over the river, oblivious to both Father and me. "I don't think I've ever seen such a view."

The opening ceremony was to be held on a Friday night, the dress rehearsal on Friday afternoon before the entire student body. The school had been readied: walls had been rubbed free of fingerprints; classes of younger children could be heard chanting recitations; the school choir, newly formed, was forever practising *"À La Claire Fontaine,"* and *"O Canada! Terre de nos aïeux,"* every recess and noon.

Because I was part of the rehearsal and opening number, I did not have to file into the gym with the rest of my class, Crawfish sidling up beside me in the line. Instead, I went through the backstage entrance, three steps up from a doorway in the hall.

Grades one to eight filed conspicuously into the gym and took their places in rows of fold-up chairs. Everyone seemed awed by the cavernous space after the one-room schools; it was still that new to us. Our little dance troupe stepped forward. The stage curtains had not yet arrived, and when I took my place at the piano and glanced at the girls lined up along the front of the stage, I saw that we were exposed like gaping fish washed up on a cliff shelf. I was glad to be on the fringes, though I could still be seen by the rows of faces that shone up like rounded buoys, from the backwaters of the darkened gym.

Each girl stood stiffly with a cane in one hand, a black top hat in the other, the hats tipped jauntily over the row of heads. Together, they were perched like thirteen Mr. Peanuts. I heard a rap on the hardwood floor, my cue from Miss Tina to play the opening bars. The sheet music was propped in front of me but when I raised my eyes all I could see were shifting lines of the same note. I felt a lightning movement inside my head. I hesitated and Miss Tina rapped again. The girls looked back over their shoulders. My hands came down on the keys, *bang bang,* and I thought, *Blind man.* I stumbled into the opening bars and made a quick decision to wing the piece by ear. I couldn't see the page anyway; it had moved away from me, in a blur.

I was aware of twenty-six feet keeping time and a chopping movement to my right, as thirteen canes axed in my direction at forty-five degrees. I had to get through the piece twice, never playing faster than the feet could *tap tap tap* and *shuffle shuffle*. As long as I did not think about separate notes, as long as I kept the rush of memory intact, my hands moved without any assistance from me. I knew that even one thought could break the flow. As soon as I thought about thinking, the thread frayed and snapped.

My hands floundered. I chorded left. My head emptied. Mind flown, memory flown. The dancers carried on, unaccompanied. I could hear the scraping of soles against dry wood. The feet stopped. I wanted to shout the way Father did, "*Keep up the beat!*" but the dancers had lost their place and so had I. The audience was still. There was no need to look out to that dark sea when I could feel it rolling up towards me in a crushing wave. I placed my hands on the keyboard and tried again, this time from the beginning. I was incapable of starting in the middle. The dancers did not move. I tried again. They made a collective decision to follow and their bodies jerked forward. I thought of thirteen Mr. Peanuts cracking open and then I tried not to think. My hands took on a speed of their own and rushed through "Pretty Baby," too quickly, two more times. The black sea inside the gym swallowed. There was a long silence during which the audience seemed to wonder whether to clap. The dancers, bewildered at this, tipped forward and left the stage. Not one of the girls looked at me.

I tried to slip out through the stage door into the hall but Miss Tina caught up with me. Behind us a row of younger children had already begun to recite, "*Dame Trot came home one wintry night, A shivering, starving soul . . .*" Miss Tina slipped an arm around my shoulder and turned me to face her. "Trude King, this is something you can do and do very well. You know it and I know it. What you probably don't know is that when we have problems in rehearsal, it's a good omen for a solid performance at night." She hugged me and I carried on, not wanting to return to the gym to join my class.

I knew now that no matter how hard I tried to lie low, I was always going to end up being a spectacle. My lungs were dry and I stepped into my room so I could be in my seat when my classmates returned. There was nowhere else to go.

But Crawfish was there before me. He was behind the door and when I opened it he moved quickly, forcing me to bump directly into his flabby chest. There were tears rolling down both blubbery cheeks.

"We've been humiliated," he said, and I felt his thick fingers groping at my bare arms. I forced myself to squint into his face.

"Oh, Trude," he said. "Of all those girls, why did it have to be you?"

I yanked away and ran for the washroom. I stayed there until I heard the school bus and then I went back for my coat and ran for it, again.

Lyd did not mention the rehearsal. Nor did Eddie, who seemed to have forgotten by the time we got home. Lyd and I were used to sharing our misery in public, now, and knew there was nothing to say. If I failed at the evening performance, the failure would be hers, too. Worse still, it would be in front of Father, whom we were forced to drag along.

I went into the clothes closet and stood between the blouses. "The hell with Crawfish," I told Mother. "I don't want him bawling on my shoulder. He won't leave me alone." My hands and arms and shoulders were knotted and tense as I went through, not every note, but every finger movement of "Pretty Baby" in my head.

We returned after supper and approached our new school, which was lit like a horizontal beacon in the dark. We had not yet had our first snowfall but I could smell its promise in the air. We'd arrived on the school bus that had been sent to St. Pierre to fetch the Protestant families for the grand opening. Parents, too, had come on the bus, riding with a grown-up air of levity that was easy to see through. I spoke to no one, but lines of one of Father's poems streamed through my head: *Into the jaws of Death, Into the mouth of Hell, Into the jaws of Death, Into the mouth of Hell.* I refused to look at Father, who was standing with the other parents, packed into the aisle. He was wearing his one brown suit and both Lyd and I tried not to acknowledge him in case he would say or do something outrageous.

We entered the school through the front door, the teachers' entrance, and I noticed that, already, the P had fallen off the wall outside, leaving ROTESTANT in its wake. A program was thrust into my hands. I'd never been to the school at night and was surprised by the artificial light illuminating the halls. Voices were not harsh the way they were during the day. The ceilings seemed low and there was a silken echo from one end of the school to the other, an atmosphere of high reverence. The teachers were dressed in fancy clothes — pleated skirts and sheer blouses — and their manners were more formal and less punitive in intent. I did not go to my room because of Crawfish. I took off my coat and handed it to Lyd. She looked as if it were she and not I who was headed for slaughter. She crushed my coat to her chest and her mouth made a kind of grimace that was meant to give me support.

The stairs inside the stage door were high and slippery with new wood. The piano looked like a piece of heavy machinery; the stool in front of it wobbled lopsidedly, something I'd never noticed before. The thirteen girls were pressed amoeba-like into the wall at one end of the stage, waiting in terror for the gym lights to go down. I did not feel my feet as I walked forward and took my place on the uneven stool. Miss Tina was calm and composed and was wearing, not her skimpy leotard, but real clothes. It was her last night in the school and she did not seem at all disturbed by the vast audience below.

But it was only *after* the performance that I remembered all of these details, not before. My pre-performance self existed in some other, closed space of its own. I played "Pretty Baby" with my eyes closed, or so I told myself at home that night, after Lyd and I had gone to bed. I had made up my mind to play well and I did. Not too quickly, no notes missed. The way I played had nothing to do with Miss Tina's kindness and nothing to do with Father's anticipatory pirouette, executed at the entrance of the school after we'd climbed down from the bus in the dark. The way I played had come out of my will. The dancers followed every beat and I knew it would be safe to face them the rest of the school year.

But when I returned home, and before I fell into bed, I walked into the empty living room and pulled the lid over the keyboard of my piano. I raised the cover of the bench and dropped in the *Play Piano* folder I'd last worked on, and on top of that, "The Whiffenpoof" and "The Midnight Fire Alarm." I could feel the weight of Father's hands on my shoulders as I closed the lid of the bench. I would not tell him my decision. Sooner or later, from my triangle of space behind the piano, I would hear what he had to say.

It was Crawfish I was going to have to deal with now. I began to steel myself for the things I would have to do to stay out of his way.

I hung my clothes in the closet and shoved aside Mother's blouses. I stood there, eyes wide open, "Pretty Baby" still rippling through my fingers and wrists. I listened to the silence of the house and thought of the thirteen dancers that evening. How they'd straightened their torsos and slid back a row of right feet in their last dying "Pretty Baby" shuffle.

GO IN AND OUT
THE WINDOW

1957

I knew Father was worried about our future when I found him at the desk in the living room altering tax receipts. On the desk were a bottle of ink remover, a dropper and a fountain pen. He was working under the glare of the gooseneck lamp and I leaned over his shoulder to watch. He placed the edge of the blotter beneath the line and changed *five* to *fifty*. The receipt had been signed, T. S. Donnell, Treasurer. Father moved the decimal, squeezed in an extra zero and blew on the paper, to dry. It was a very professional job.

"Isn't that cheating?" I said. "Dad?"

"Louis St. Laurent is still eating rare roast beef and mushrooms on my taxes," he said. "Duplessis isn't showing any signs of quitting, either." He was not in a good mood.

I went out to the kitchen and found Lyd dyeing her shoes. One arm and both hands were blotched with canary yellow shoe dye. She held the dauber upside down.

"Leo wants me to go to the dance tonight," I said. "He has a date for you."

"No," she said. "Definitely not."

"His friend is tall."

"No."

"Well then, give me a reason."

"I can give you more than one," she said. "I'll give you two. I hate blind dates, and you'd be lying. Father would kill us both if he knew you were lying."

"It's not a blind date. Leo knows him. He isn't going to bring someone you'll hate. And I'll tell Father I'll be with you. The truth."

"Partial truth."

"It's a stupid rule, Lyd. If I'm with you or a bunch of girls from school, I can go. If a guy asks me out, I'm not allowed."

"Not my rule," said Lyd.

"I'm not staying home. Anyway, I need you to do something with my hair."

From the way she looked up I knew she sympathized. During the week, I'd chopped my own hair trying to make myself look older, and had made a real mess of it. I'd never done that before.

I thought of Leo then, how he and I danced together, and I added, "You can wear your canary yellow shoes."

With this, we both snorted with laughter. The day before, we'd taken the bus to Hull and crossed the river to Ottawa to shop in the only store that sold women's shoes, size ten and up. Although it was a store we hated, it was not without interest.

It was a small narrow shop with displays lining the side walls, nothing longer than a size nine in sight. Everything else was hidden away. The all-male sales staff greeted women as they slipped in and out of the Sparks Street entrance. A bell tinkled overhead every time an oversized foot pressed the welcome mat at the door.

Lyd and I were ignored but we'd braced ourselves; we'd been there the summer before and we'd been ignored then, too. We walked around the edges of the shop, keeping an eye on women in matching suits, purses and gloves. We did not know who they were but, clearly, *they* were rich and we were not. We were there only because of the size of Lyd's feet, and because she'd saved enough babysitting money for one pair of shoes.

The oversize shoes were discreetly stacked in towers of boxes behind what Lyd and I called the *Curtain of Dread*. Eventually, an older man came over, took a look at the two of us, took a look at Lyd's feet and pointed to a chair. "Kick up the pumps, kid," he said, and held out his hand for her foot. That really set us off.

The reason I was with Lyd in the first place was because it was unthinkable for her to be in this store alone. If humiliation was going to fall her way, we would share it. Over the past year and a half we had devised a repertoire of foot-and-height rituals that we carried out every time we were in town. It was my responsibility to walk on the inside because sidewalks slanted downward towards the curb and Lyd felt shorter on the outside. If I forgot, she hissed and rushed around behind me. We knew we would have to keep up this behaviour until her feet and the rest of her body stopped growing but we had no way of knowing when that would be.

"Don't work on me, Trude," she said now. "You know I

hate the dances on Skinner's Road. I always end up with the one guy who comes up to my armpits. Tell me why the shortest guys ask the tallest girls to dance. Tell me that."

"Maybe they never had Mommies," I said. But the remark had flown out of me before I could stop it.

We never talked about the *details* of Mother, the reminders of the *life* of her. We'd never given away the special dresses, the hand-sewn ones that still hung in the long closet in plastic wardrobes. Or the brush-and-mirror set that had been cleared off the top of her vanity and crammed into a bottom drawer. We didn't speak of the way she'd never gone out without first putting on a pair of earrings or a pair of white gloves, even to take the bus to town to get groceries at the A&P. Or the time she hauled the Queen Anne chairs and the Tiffany lamps and the kitchen set down to the riverbank, chopped them up and burned them because she wanted something new, of her own.

"Do you think we don't have enough money?" I asked Lyd.

"We don't have two cents," she said. She sounded like our mother when she said that. She even looked like our mother.

"Not us. I mean the family, Father. He's cheating on next year's tax receipts in the other room."

"I don't want to hear it," she said. "I absolutely do not want to hear it." She stood up and dangled two brilliant yellow shoes from her index fingers. "Done," she said, and held them out for me to see. These were the shoes we'd come away with the day before, the one and only pair the salesman had carried out from behind the *Curtain of Dread*. They were flats, straw flats. Yesterday, they'd been mauve. Lyd had not expected them to fit and they hadn't. She'd paid up and we'd run out the door and kept on running for two blocks until we reached the corner of O'Connor. We'd stood in front of Zellers, gasping for breath until we calmed down.

"We're cursed," Lyd said. "The females in this family are doomed to have big feet." I didn't agree because I was pretty sure mine had stopped growing, but I didn't say anything. Then we went inside, and Lyd picked out the canary yellow shoe dye.

I began to work on her again. With or without permission, I was going to the dance. It would be a lot easier to get past Father if Lyd and I were to leave the house together. But Lyd liked to stay home.

Father and I — I wasn't sure how this had come about — had begun to set up resistance to each other. No matter how small the issue, our wills collided. He didn't seem to be able to deal with the fact that Lyd and I were turning ourselves into women — though she and I never talked about or even spoke the word. It was like being on an unstoppable journey, heading into future unknown without parental approval. If Father had noticed that we were growing up, he wasn't letting on. Lyd and he were okay, and Eddie managed to stay out of his way, but sometimes he and I would look each other in the eye and anger would erupt. He was trying to keep me back, I thought; he was trying to hold me down in childhood forever.

I remembered a prediction Mother had made on my tenth birthday. "You," she said. "Just wait till you're in your headstrong years. Your fighting spirit will rear up from its hiding place and come rushing out, just like your father's. I never saw a child so strong-willed." But even as she'd warned, I'd felt her yield to the complicitous weave of genes. Wills. One will rising to meet another. Nothing could prevent that.

Lyd surprised me suddenly and gave in. It was an unexpected collapse of *her* will. She pushed a foot into one yellow shoe and stood in the middle of the kitchen and took the shoe off again.

"All right," she said. "I'll go. But this is the last time I'll be your cover. Get the scissors and I'll start working on your hair."

Though Leo and I liked to dance together, most of our conversation was about his car. He had quit school two years earlier and bought an old green Pontiac. It needed so much work I knew there would never be an end to it. Already, he'd done fender repairs, paint job, had added secondhand tires and a furry beige cover that stretched across the front seat. Leo was five years older than I, the reason I had to keep him away from Father. He was also teaching me to drive. When we were in the car together on country roads, I slid over beside him and shifted gears while he took care of the clutch. Twice, when there'd been no traffic, I'd climbed across and taken over the wheel completely. I couldn't get my licence for another year and a half, but by then I planned to be an expert driver.

Lyd did not approve of Leo. Too old, she said. Watch out for him. And dumb sideburns. Temperamental about his car, too. What I hadn't told her was that he'd begun to collect glasses and saucers and cups at the drive-in movies, and that these were stored in a cardboard box in the trunk of his car. He'd talked to me about wanting four little red-haired children but it had never occurred to me that he had me in mind as their future mother. I didn't have so much as a streak of red in my hair and neither did he. There was simply no connection.

One afternoon when he picked me up at my high school he

let me have a glimpse of a photo he held in one palm and quickly covered over with the other. It was a photo of a pyramid of adult bodies, all naked. Each naked body was doing something to the one on top and the one below. I was shocked by the photo but my reaction only made Leo laugh. He had taken the photo from his father's collection at home, he said, and would have to put it back. I was too young to have a second look, he told me. He pressed his hands against my hips. "What the girls in the picture know is how to wiggle these," he said.

Another day, he told me that once the work on his car was finished, he was going to save to buy an old farm. When he had enough money, he would start to fix *that* up.

I knew there were people like Leo and my childhood friend, Mimi, who seemed to know what their future would be and then shaped themselves to fit the plan. But when I looked into my own future I could see nothing ahead but space. I didn't know what Lyd would do, but *my* plan was to get out of St. Pierre as soon as I finished school. I had no idea what would happen after that. The plan, if there was one, was simply to leave.

I didn't see Mimi often any more but Lyd and I had met her on the bus when we were coming home late from school one Friday afternoon, at the beginning of May. We had boarded the bus on Taché Boulevard near the Standish; we'd moved to the long seat across the back, and there she was.

Mimi was only a year older than I but already she looked older than Lyd. She'd quit school in the village after Christmas and now worked as a filing clerk for the government, in Ottawa. She'd had to lie about her age, she said; she and her mother had fixed her birth certificate.

She was wearing a shiny green dress that was sheath tight,

and three-inch black patent heels. She wore large earrings and long beads that made me think of the rosary I'd once painted and that we'd buried beside the river. We'd never gone back to dig it up. Seven or eight bracelets clattered up and down her arms and as they slid over her bones I caught a glimpse of tiny wrists. She was wearing eggshell make-up and I could see the line where it ended, along the side of her neck. Lyd and I were allowed to wear lipstick, that was all.

When we got off at the same stop in the village, she invited me to come over. "We hardly ever see each other now that you go to school in Hull," she said. "Grand-mère misses you. My mother, too. She can't get a divorce, you know, and that's sad. We don't even know where Bee-Bee lives. My mother's appendix nearly burst last year because we couldn't find him to sign the consent. Well, never mind, he put in a bathroom before he left. *Mes tantes* stood around the bowl and took turns flushing." A sharp laugh came out of her and for a moment she seemed on the verge of hysteria. "Anyway," she said, "come over some weekend and I'll show you what I've collected for my hope chest. Every pay, I buy one new thing. Last pay it was a cigarette box from Tunisia. With a lid. Next month I'm buying a pair of baby dolls at Murphy's — they're black, mostly black lace."

I thought of Lyd and me and our shared dresser and how we swapped clothes for school — Kitten sweater sets, mostly Orlon. And cinch belts, hair bands and short-sleeved blouses. The thought of either of us having a hope chest, or black baby-doll pyjamas from Murphy Gamble on Sparks Street, was preposterous.

Lyd and I spent most of the afternoon sitting on the edge of the bed, playing "I Almost Lost My Mind," over and over on the record player, wailing along with Pat Boone while we did things to ourselves. Lyd evened out the sides of my chopped hair but couldn't get the back the way she wanted. "I give up," she said. "I can't fix it." She dug into her top drawer and held up the fake ponytail she'd bought at the Metropolitan in Hull at the beginning of June. The match was perfect for my own dark hair but when she pinned it on I felt as if something free-floating and unnatural had been attached to my skull. I didn't want to wear it but I didn't have much choice.

"Leo will never know it isn't yours," said Lyd. "Nobody will. You can't even see the pins."

I moved to the right and the hair shifted side to side. I moved forward and back and reached up to check that it was still attached.

"Don't touch," she said. "If you do, you'll loosen it. It'll be perfectly okay if you keep your hands *off*."

We took a blanket to the backyard and stretched out to tan our legs in the last rays of the afternoon sun.

Ten minutes later, I sat up in disbelief. I'd heard the unmistakable nasal voice of Kitty Wells singing "Searching." Leo was driving right up to the front of the house, windows down, radio full blast.

"For God's sake," I said, "Leo must be crazy. He's driving up to the front door. Run around the side of the house, quick, Lyd, find out what's going on. For God's sake, does he think Father's going to want to *meet* him?" I tore down to the end of the yard as if that would distance me from Leo's behaviour. Lyd disappeared around the corner of the house.

Not a minute later I watched the Pontiac turn away from the river and head back towards the village. Lyd returned, her face white, her lips set like the grim messenger she was.

"Father told him to come back in twenty years," she said. "Leo said he wanted to take you to the dance. He said he intended to pick you up at the front door and Father said, 'Fat chance.' That's when he told him to come back in twenty years. Leo's such a lout," she added. "You'd think he'd have asked before coming here. Didn't you tell him what Father is like?"

Father came to the back door and stood behind the screen looking out as if he were ready for a fight. "You won't be going out of this house tonight," he said. "Either one of you. And I don't want to hear two words about it."

"I'm not a baby!" I yelled at him from the yard. I thought he would tear down the steps after me, but he didn't. "I'm old enough to go out!" I yelled again. He stared at me for a moment and then turned and disappeared into the shadows of the summer kitchen.

"You're lucky he didn't come out," Lyd said. "The ponytail saved you. I think he was trying to figure out what was different. Anyway, that settles that. We won't be at the dance tonight." She sounded relieved that she didn't have to go.

Technically, by Father's own rules, we knew that Lyd could go if she wanted to. She was already sixteen. While one part of me raged at the injustice, another part thought, He'll never keep me in. It isn't fair and there's nothing wrong with going to a dance on Saturday night and all my friends will be there and if he won't let me go, I'll run away. I felt so weightless inside this decision, I wondered why I'd never thought of it before. But I had to take Lyd; I knew I couldn't run away alone.

It was after nine and the dance had started but Lyd and I were still in our room, waiting for Father to fall asleep in his maroon chair in the living room. By the time the front of the house was silent, it was quarter to ten. We set the radio volume low and turned out the light and humped pillows under the bedclothes. I'd been working on Lyd for hours and we were both strained and exhausted from the effort. Not only that, we were petrified. This was our greatest act of defiance, and even though we were running away we knew that wherever we would run, Father would find us. He would track us down and there would be some unknown consequence that none of us, not even Father, had ever had to imagine.

It wasn't difficult to tumble out the bedroom window; we'd been doing it all our lives. Father had sprung fire drills throughout our entire childhood and we'd learned to leap in and out of the bungalow windows from every part of the house. At the last minute, though we hadn't done any planning, Lyd turned back and riffled through the closet and hauled out her long blue winter coat. When we reached the main road, we checked our pockets. Between us we had two quarters, two Smith Brothers cough drops and the blue coat. Lyd was wearing her canary yellow shoes. The fake ponytail was swinging behind me, and I kept putting my hand up to check that it was still there. I wondered if Leo would notice, and then I didn't care. I was furious at him *and* my Father. No one owns me, I thought. Not Father and not Leo. It's all Leo's fault in the first place that Lyd and I have to run away. We could have gone out to meet our girlfriends and somebody would have given us a ride to the dance later, and Father would never have known.

We headed out of the village but the first time we heard a car behind us, we jumped down into the roadside ditch. Father didn't own a car, and even though it was unlikely that he was out of his chair, I couldn't help imagining possible scenarios: Father running through the house like a chicken with its head cut off. Father calling his old friend Roy and shouting into the phone like a madman. The two men jumping into Roy's big car, its searchlights roving the night trying to pick out canary yellow shoes or two hunched backs in the ditch. Our plan was to get out of the village and phone Leo from the crossroads, a mile away. There was a small restaurant there, called Herbie's, a few tables inside and a pay phone outside. We'd get change for one of our quarters and call the dance hall, where I was pretty sure Leo would be waiting. There were always people hanging out by the pay phone there, and everyone knew the number. I imagined what my friends from school would say.

Lyd and Trude have run away.

Oh my God, you're kidding. Their Father will kill them.

They're on their way here. They want Leo to go to Herbie's to pick them up.

Trude's not supposed to go out. Her father's really strict — especially since their mother died.

Their mother drowned, you know, the year before last.

I know that. They're practically orphans.

If they've run away, where will they run to after the dance?

This was something we hadn't considered. I'd been reluctant to bring it up in case Lyd changed her mind. As it was, her enthusiasm had begun to wither. When I went inside and sat down after phoning, she said, "I think we'd better go home." She said it flatly, using her older-sister voice. "I don't care if Father kills us."

"We can't go home. How can you come this far and give up? What's the matter with you? We've already walked — run — more than a mile."

"The dance is the first place Father is going to look," Lyd said. "That moron Leo might as well have broadcast it to the whole world."

"Well, he's on his way. And he's bringing your date. We can't go home now." I tried to compromise. "We'll go for two dances and turn around and come right back."

"Forget it," said Lyd. "I don't want the blind date any more. I never did. This is the stupidest thing we've ever done. *Look at me!*" she shouted. She pointed to smudges on her skirt, to the dirt on her yellow shoes. We'd been in and out of the ditch four times. The winter coat was heaped beside her on the seat.

"Look at *me*, why don't you!" I shouted back. We were half-laughing, half-crying. But Lyd was right. This was the stupidest thing we'd ever done. And it was true that Father was going to kill us.

I didn't tell Lyd that Leo and I had fought, over the phone. He was angry about Father turning him away and he wasn't happy about leaving the dance to come back to get me. It was almost ten-thirty and the dance would end at midnight. In the time it would take him to come back for us and drive there again, we'd be lucky to be there for twenty minutes.

"I ran away so I could meet you," I'd said into the phone. I thought I was going to cry. "I'm in a lot of trouble."

"I didn't ask you to run away," he said. He definitely sounded chilly.

"What about Lyd's date? Where's he?"

"He's with someone else. I don't think he'll want to leave now."

"You'd better bring someone," I shouted. "We're at Herbie's and we're going to wait fifteen minutes and after that, the hell with you!" I slammed down the phone and went back inside.

Leo screeched into Herbie's parking lot and spun the wheels. There was someone in the back of the car and as soon as Lyd and I saw his head we knew he was going to be short.

"Jesus Poêle!" Lyd said. "Who's that?"

His name was Willard and he was five inches shorter than Lyd. This didn't seem to bother him at all and he grinned as he jumped out and opened the back door.

Halfway in, I smelled something as I slid across the front seat. The radio was tuned to the cowboy station, pounding at top volume. Leo was staring straight ahead. There was a brown bag on the floor, at his feet. As soon as we shut the doors he swerved onto the road and hit the gas pedal. Right away Lyd said, "Don't go so fast."

I turned around and saw her at one end of the seat, Willard at the other, the winter coat between them. Leo leaned forward and then handed the brown bag over the back of the seat.

"You guys aren't supposed to be drinking in the car," Lyd said. "If you're going to drink, let me out."

We were on country road now, a long dark stretch between farms. It was a road we knew well because for years we'd been bussed this way to one-room schools during our elementary grades. The dance hall was still a couple of miles away.

"Slow down," Lyd said. "I told you I want out. Tell him to slow down," she said to me.

Leo reached back for the brown bag and steered with one hand. I'd never noticed before how thick his neck was, how square his jaw. *Wills*, I thought. Now it's Leo's will, set against the rest of us. The words *cradle robber* jumped into my head and I stared at him as if he'd just swooped down to Earth to scoop me up. I had a sudden urge to tell Lyd about the box of cups and saucers multiplying in the trunk but I didn't dare turn around. I wanted Lyd to shut up because she was making matters worse. I wanted to get to the dance hall, have our two dances and leave, though I had no idea where we'd go after that.

A momentary image of Father tracking us flitted through my mind. Maybe he'd gone past while we were at Herbie's and he was already at the dance. Maybe he'd alerted the village policeman, old *Rouge Gorge* with the tin star. Maybe he was just waking up now, in the maroon chair. But somehow, I couldn't put him through the next moves. I could not create a picture of him opening our bedroom door, pushing at the lumps under the covers, suspicious because Lyd and I had gone to bed early. I could not put a face or an expression to these acts. I could only see the back of his head, hear his knuckles tapping at our bedroom door.

We were coming to the one long curve on Skinner's Road. There was a black barn on the left, a dairy farm at the end of a lane on the right.

"Don't be a jerk!" Lyd shouted from behind. "You're going too fast. Stop the damn car!"

Leo pressed his foot to the gas pedal in response, and passed the brown bag to Willard just as we entered the curve. And lost control. We went into a long skid on the wrong side of the road and sudden startling headlights exploded in our faces. Leo jammed the brakes and my body lifted forward. As I bumped the mirror I felt his hand reach out and grab my head from behind. I flew back against the seat and stayed there.

We were tilted in the ditch, and though the car was terrifyingly still I could hear sounds of shifting gravel. The other car had landed in the opposite ditch, each car having displaced the other without touching. A man and woman Father's age were coming towards us. They were holding on to each other and seemed to be walking and walking but never reaching our side of the road. I looked to my left and saw Lyd outside the car holding her coat and one yellow shoe. Her mouth was open and she was banging the shoe against the window on Leo's side as if she were going to use it to kill him. She hurled it over the top of the car and it disappeared into the night. My head moved towards Leo then, and I saw him staring down into his right hand. He was holding something that looked like black fur and he was clearly astonished and horrified by what he saw. I couldn't make out what it was but some part of me recognized my ponytail just as he began to shout. He was shaking his hand as if the thing were alive, and he dropped the fistful of hair to the floor. Willard was at the side window, peering back into the car. I hadn't heard either him or Lyd get out. We were alive, all of us. The man and woman were still walking towards us, even though their car wasn't more than thirty feet away. I couldn't stop seeing events as unconnected parts. Sounds were tunnelled and delayed. Anything I might have known before this moment seemed far away and lost.

And then, everything speeded up. Leo was out of the car. I slid under the steering wheel and he pulled me up to the rim of the ditch. My head felt lighter. I kept rubbing my fingers against the bump on my forehead. Voices were shouting. Willard was pounding his fist against the rear fender. Threats and accusations were hurled. Lyd was begging the man and woman to drive us home. Leo fell silent and stared off into space.

"He's in shock," the woman said. "He's all right. Let someone else come and pull him out of the ditch." She was furious. Her husband went back across the road and managed to back his own car out with ease. It didn't seem to be damaged, although there was dust on the doors and windshield. He rolled down the window and called out, "I've got your licence, buddy. You were doing double speed. You'll be lucky I don't report you to the police. It's a miracle we're alive, every one of us."

His wife said, "Come on, girls, get in the back. What on earth are you doing with someone who drives like that, and at this time of night? Your mothers would have a fit. Do they know where you are? Tell us where you live and we'll take you home."

"Our mother is dead," Lyd said. She said it just like that. "We live with our father. We're sisters and we live in the same house."

I could not think where that might be.

Lyd gave directions from the back seat and spread the winter coat over the two of us, tucking in the edges. As we drove away, I turned. I saw Leo looking down at Willard and Willard looking up at Leo as if they'd never before seen each other, as if they'd found themselves together in a ditch on a new planet, a place they were visiting for the first time.

"Awwh, for God's sake, these girls don't have a mother," the woman said. Her hand reached towards and then pulled away from her husband's shoulder. He was holding the steering wheel so tightly his knuckles shone white, even in the interior darkness of the car. There was silence and then she said, between her teeth, "No wonder. But if those two young men had been sons of mine, I'd have knocked their blocks off. I smelled liquor, too. Did you smell liquor?" But her husband didn't answer.

When we reached our dirt road by the river, it occurred to me to remember that we were fugitives returned. A long time ago, we'd been ordinary sisters living in this house. The man insisted on driving us to the door and even offered to speak to Father, but we persuaded him that we weren't hurt at all. I looked boldly at him as if daring him to get out of the car. "Our father goes to bed early," I said. "He doesn't like us to wake him." I could see a lamp shining from the living room as I spoke. "Thanks for driving us home."

The porch was silent. The front of the house looked the same as always. Lyd and I stood still, expecting Father to burst through the door and come roaring down the steps. Nothing happened. We waited a few more seconds and then, instinctively, we crouched down and ran along the side of the house. We'd left the window open and now Lyd shoved the blue coat at me and climbed. Inside, she listened, put a finger to her lips and reached down to haul me up. When I got over the sill I saw that she was wearing only one shoe. She took it off and lowered it to the wastebasket.

Something was lifting. I dared to feel safety, mercy, acquittal, release. We stripped off our clothes and dropped them to the floor and slipped into our big double bed. As if the moment had been choreographed, we heard Father stir in his chair and walk through the front of the house as he turned out the lights and went to his room.

"You didn't get your other shoe," I whispered. "It landed in the field."

"I don't care," said Lyd. "I hate the damn shoes anyway."

"We could find it if we went back," I said. "It would glow in the dark."

We tried to laugh but we couldn't.

"We'll have to go back to the *Curtain of Dread*," Lyd said. "When I save enough money. You're coming with me."

"I know," I said.

It was only when I started to tell her about Leo staring into the fistful of black hair that we began to let go. We shook with hysteria and mourned the ponytail, and Lyd made me describe, over and over, the look on Leo's face as he dropped what he must have believed was my scalp, which lay curled like a dead animal on the car floor. We laughed about Willard coming up to Lyd's armpit, and how it was a good thing she hadn't had to lead him around the dance floor. We laughed about plates being the next bonus at the drive-in, how Leo would soon have a set of four to place before his square-jawed children who would never look like me. But even while we laughed, we did not gloat. We did not once mention the rules of the house, and we did not mention running away. We had got away with something very big and we knew this. And we knew, as we fell into silence, that what we had got away with had nothing to do with the way we had deceived our father.

INTERPROVINCIAL

1959

The wind roared in our ears all the way home from Darley. Father refused to shut his window and said he had to have air. Eddie was riding shotgun. The window on his side was down, too. Lyd and I tried to lip-read in the back; we couldn't hear a thing over the wind.

"It's no use," her lips exaggerated. She had to form the words three times before I understood. Then we got into it.

"He's upset," I mouthed. "The funeral."

"He's always upset these days," said Lyd's lips. "Weird." She jabbed a finger into the back of the driver's seat and made twirling motions. The inside of our Chevy was turquoise, even the back of the seats. It was our first car. It was one year old and it had fins.

"I felt that," said Father. "Cut it out, whatever you're doing back there."

"Did he cry?" I asked Lyd. I dragged two fingers down my cheeks.

"Don't think so," said the lips.

The call had come while we were at supper. The Giant Ant in tears; Grampa King, dead. We sat in silence and listened to Father's side of the conversation.

Grampa's heart had stopped after he'd done a day's work. He'd eaten his supper and was sitting in his chair about to darn a pair of wool socks. He'd put the darning egg inside the sock and dropped the sock to the floor. When Uncle Ewart heard the crack he looked up. Grampa King had leaned into his chair, dead.

"Egg?" Father said into the phone. "Darning egg?"

At the funeral parlour, Father and Uncle Ewart, the Giant Ant and Uncle Wash, were directed to an alcove that faced the coffin; *their* grief was meant to be separate. The rest of us sat in pews in the main room, also facing the coffin. Granny Tracks had come, "Out of respect," she told us, and sat beside me, scrunching my right hand between both of hers. Lorne, the hired hand, was in the pew behind. The room was filled with people I didn't know; there were men standing at the back. Grampa King had been dressed in a navy-blue suit and there was a red splotch over one eyebrow. His hair was neat and I thought he'd been made to look like an imposter. For one thing, he'd never worn anything but overalls. I was pleased to see that beneath his top shirt button, a safety pin was holding him together.

When it was time to close the coffin just before the service began, a curtain was pulled across the alcove so the eyes of

Father and Uncle Ewart and the Giant Ant would not see the lid coming down on their father. Granny Tracks had taken a dizzy spell at that very moment and I had to help her outside so she could breathe. Lorne followed us out. The three of us sat on the steps and missed most of my grandfather's funeral. We got to hear the last hymn when Lorne propped a stone to hold the door ajar. Everyone inside was singing "How sweet the hour of closing day." Lorne and Granny hummed in harmony until the *Amen*.

I'd been to one funeral before, and that was Mother's. The memory I held of that was of Rebecque's voice overhead, telling me what to do. The kindness of her had kept us all moving. We'd had to drive through Hull in a long black car, following the hearse from the church to the graveyard, up the hill. The car had moved so slowly and smoothly I kept thinking we weren't moving. My entire Sunday school class had been at the service, and most of my classmates from St. Pierre, too. There had been no place to get away; we just had to keep moving.

"The head has many aches," Granny Tracks said, and she pulled herself up from the top step and brushed her dress. Her face looked as if it had been chalked. Lorne nodded in gloom. We went back into the funeral parlour, past the door with the removable sign that said *Whitley King*. I did not believe that *that* Whitley King was my grandfather.

When we returned to the farm to eat and drink, Uncle Ewart called Lyd and me and Eddie upstairs to Grampa's room. He raised the lid of the trunk at the foot of Grampa's bed and lifted out a heavy Bible.

"This was your grandmother's," he said. "It's been in the trunk all these years. I don't think your Grampa ever took it out. There isn't anyone here who walks through a church door more than twice a year, Christmas and Easter, sometimes not even Easter, so you'd better take it home with you."

He handed the Bible to Lyd because she was the eldest. It was worn along the edges and had a pebbled black cover. I looked at Uncle Ewart, who seemed big and uncomforted, and I thought of how he listened to "Ol' Man River" on Grampa's wind-up gramophone, and how every night after supper he washed down his food with a glass of milk from his own cow.

Lyd had the Bible open in the back seat while Father raced through one Ontario town after another, heading for Quebec. He wanted to get home before dark. He'd missed two days' work but could not take a third because of his new job. "Can't take the chance," he said. "I've been at it less than a year. Those people in Ottawa want to know that I'll show up."

Father now worked in a glass tower at a big General Motors car dealer across the Interprovincial Bridge, in downtown Ottawa. He told us that bookkeeping was better than munitions and trays any day.

"My intimate relations with the fleurs-de-lis have ended," he announced, the day the factory closed in the village. "The postwar prosperity I've been reading about all these years has not dipped down to the bottom of Quebec. Darkness encroaching," he added. "Tunnel narrowing, ahead." Then he and Duffy disappeared to the hotel and stayed out half the night.

Father was without work only four days. The car dealer needed a bookkeeper to replace the one they'd just fired because the accounts had been jimmied. Father heard about the job on a Saturday, when he was riding the bus.

He needed a car to get back and forth to Ottawa because he said he couldn't breathe through the dust that rose up through the bus floors. The past winter, he'd bought a '57 Chevy off the used-car lot; the used-car manager told him that in its first year and a half it had been owned by two nuns. I had my learner's permit now but I could already drive. I was just waiting for my birthday so I could get my licence in the summer. Lyd said she didn't want a licence. She didn't care if she ever drove.

She knocked me in the ribs and pointed to the King Bible. "Look," said her lips. "Read."

In the centre were two pages marked *Family Register*. On the left someone had filled in the birthdates of Aunt Lucy, Uncle Ewart and Father. It was not easy to imagine the event of Father's birth. Beside Father's date, a note had been added: *Born with a caul*.

Lyd raised her eyebrows and mouthed, "What?"

I read the entry again and shrugged. She put her finger to her lips and rolled her eyes in Father's direction. "Don't even ask," said the silent voice.

Born with a caul. I said it over and over to myself but could not make sense of it. I closed my eyes so I wouldn't have to read Lyd's lips any more. Instead, I thought of Grampa King in his navy suit. I tried to think back and remember him the way he'd been, a long time ago, when we'd moved away from Darley.

We had stood on the platform at the station, the train puffing beside us. Both sides of the family had been there to see us off. Granny Tracks had clutched Mother as if we were moving two thousand and not two hundred miles away.

"Can you say any French words?" Grampa King had asked. "You'll have to learn *oui* and *non*."

"I know more complicated words than that," I told him. "I've been practising. No one in Darley knows one word of French so

I've been teaching it to myself. You run the words together fast until they sound like this: Blah-blah-blah-blah-blah."

"I know *ooo la la*," said Grampa King, over my head. He was staring into the vanishing point in the tracks. "I learned it in the First Great War. That is also the place I learned the gesture of hands." He looked down at his own.

The train was making jerking noises and we raised our feet to the steps and climbed aboard. When we were all inside I lowered my window and stuck out an arm, ready to wave. We were so high up, Granny Tracks looked small standing on the platform below. She glared meaningfully at me. "You and your sister prepare yourselves to mind your p's and q's when you grow up," she said.

The train answered with a rush of steam.

"*Ooo la la!*" I shouted down to Grampa King. "Blah-blah-blah-blah-blah!"

"Shut the window," Father said. He'd settled into the seat facing me and Eddie. Lyd was sitting with Mother across the aisle. Mother had turned away from us and Lyd was pretending that she was not part of the King family on the move. Soot was pouring in and already Eddie's face and mine were smudged with black.

"Shut the damned window," Father had said, again. "Just try to stay clean, will you, until we get to your new home."

Well, I thought. I opened my eyes. Grampa King is under the ground and I hardly know anything else about him except that he was silent most of the time, and his favourite radio program used to be "Jake and the Kid."

Our family is shrinking, I thought. And now I'm a traveller

in my father's first car and we've been living in Quebec for years and I know hundreds of French words, maybe even thousands, if I counted them up.

As if he could read my mind, Eddie began to sing in French, from the front seat. He quickly switched songs.

> *Alouettey*
> Smoke a cigarettey
> Chew tobaccy
> Spitty on the floor

No one was in the mood.

"Enough!" Father said.

"I don't think I can stand one more thing going wrong in this family," said Lyd. "Father's getting more weird by the day."

She had come home early from business school in Ottawa where she was learning shorthand. I loved the swirls and curves and lines of it. She'd showed me how to write my name — a right-leaning *w* with a fallen side, the other side shooting off into the air.

Lyd had a grey suit now, which she'd bought at Middleman's. She wore it with black shoes, flats. The suit had a straight jacket and two pleats at the waist of the skirt. I teased her about looking "office proper." The business school taught her that her hair was supposed to be up, too. And how to dress when she went to apply for a job.

I was about to graduate from grade eleven, high school leaving in Quebec. In the fall I planned to move to British Columbia.

I was going to get a job for the summer, save the fare, cross the whole vast country sitting up in a train — no berth — and find work in Vancouver. I knew Father would say I was too young but I was prepared to fight him when I was ready. It wasn't my fault Quebec schools had only eleven grades. Anyway, I planned to live safely at the "Y" in Vancouver until I got on my feet.

I was off for five days, now, because it was review week before exams. I'd been peeling potatoes when Lyd came in. We took turns making supper before Eddie came home from his paper route, and Father from work.

"What do you mean, things are weird?" I said.

"After we go to bed," Lyd said, "Father writes things. I got up last night to see who was in the living room. Whatever he had in front of him, he tried to cover over. It was two o'clock in the morning."

I knew Father had been getting up in the night, leaving for work earlier than usual, spending more and more time alone when he was home. Sometimes he went to the Pines — to the cliff overlooking the headwaters of the rapids — and stood there as if awaiting a sign. Other times he marauded up and down the banks, stepping over heaps of drift logs that had washed to shore. Occasionally he and Duffy rowed upriver to fish, one at the oars, the other at the prow to call out deadheads — the log drive had been heavy this year. Most of the time, Father was pulling more and more into himself. All of this made me more determined to get away.

"I have to study for finals, Lyd. I don't want to stay in high school the rest of my life. Anyway, I can't solve Father's problems. I'm getting out of here, remember?"

"Then you'd better tell Father your plans," she said. "Anyway, I'm only mentioning it. He *is* our father."

"It's the grief," I said. "Mother died. His father died. Even if there *is* something else, what would we do?"

"We could try to find out what that something else is," she said.

I looked at her and groaned. We walked into the living room, checked the desk, checked the shelves. Went to his bedroom and pulled out the heavy mahogany drawers. At the bottom we found a thick Hilroy scribbler with times tables on the back. Inside the cover Father had written: *Private journal of Jock King*. None of the entries was dated, except for an occasional day of the week.

> Tuesday: Five-thirty, tidied desk in tower. Walked downstairs and through showroom. Aware of an increase in pulse. Didn't think much about it, opened car door in staff parking lot and slipped behind wheel. By the time I reached Sussex St. and curved down to the bridge, was perspiring and grabbing at my collar. Loosened the knot of my tie. Hands clammy at the wheel. Sucked air when the tires bumped onto the planks of the bridge. Could feel and hear the rattle and echo of wood. Heart fluttered like wings in a cage. Was certain I'd black out.

"Jesus Cripes," said Lyd. "He's sick."

"Wait a minute," I said. "Keep reading."

We took turns and read aloud to each other.

> Wednesday: River calm. Left early. The drive to Ottawa, no problem. But can't get home at night. Can't seem to get across the Interprovincial Bridge.

In my head, the picture of black black water. Know its distance beneath the bridge, know its depth and speed of flow. Dare not look down. Tonight when I reached the Hull side, careened to the right and parked at edge of road. Had to get out. Leaned into car roof and knew I'd never cross again. Logic denies this. Have to cross again. How else to feed my children? How else to get home?

"This is like a book," I said.

"Or something very strange," said Lyd.

"Hurry up and read," I said, "or Father will be home from work. If he can *get* home."

"This might have been written weeks ago," she said. "There are no dates, remember?"

"But you said he was writing last night."

"Well, there's more."

Thursday: Walked to shore, sat on bank, stared at Ontario — far far away. Miles downriver, three bridges link Ontario to Quebec. Past the rapids, past the booms. Three ways to cross.

Checked to make sure children weren't around, closed eyes, traced route in my head, starting at dirt road in front of house. Theory: If trip can be done in the mind's eye, panic can be overcome on the bridge.

Begin: Follow pocked road out of village; turn right onto lower gravel road, follow river's flow, catch glints of blue through scrub. Pass turn-off to first bridge, the Champlain. Long slow curve of lampposts, Chinese restaurant below, mild ripple of white water all around.

Carry on to Moussette Park where my children roller skate; through Val Tétreau, up hill, down again, pass the graveyard, Armories, cross the tracks, pass the Standish Hall and into downtown Hull. Peer inside E. B. Eddy building through stick-propped windows; glimpse men in undershirts guiding thunderous rolls of paper. Ignore turn-off to Chaudière Bridge with old timber slides and falls.

Keep going: past Fortin Gravelle, past Ottawa House, bump over cobbles of Main Street of Hull. Waver in and out of streetcar tracks, see Achbar Furniture, St. James Anglican, the Laurier Theatre where children aren't allowed to go. Pass the Interprovincial Hotel on the Quebec side, below. Salute, and cross the bridge. Carry on to my place of work.

No change of heart rate.

No shortness of breath.

Now. Return journey. Have to take the head journey home.

Lock door of office. Place one foot before the other, descend tower stairs. Identify sleek sharp fins of Chevy in the lot, rub sleeve over hood rockets, for luck, unlock door.

So far, okay.

Turn wheels away from lot; hands start to tingle, then feet. Blood rushes from my head; dizziness between the ears.

Can't do it. Can't get myself home.

Even in imagination, can't drive onto bridge and reach the other side. Cannot turn the car homeward, to Quebec.

Lyd passed the scribbler to me and I read.

Friday: After they left for school, I circled back and came home. Went to shore and dipped hands in river. Thought of Maura and wondered what I'd say if I could speak to her now. Would I tell her that I carried on? Every fleur-de-lis etched onto aluminum placed a slice of pea-meal bacon on our plates. I carried on, though the girls don't use the trays, now, in our own home. Carried on until last year, when the machines in the factory were silenced and every man walked away.

I'd tell Maura that I have my first shirt-and-tie job. Keeping books in an office in a glass tower that overlooks a showroom of waxed-and-polished cars. That we have our first car, a '57 Chevy with fins — two-tone blue, storm and sky. When I saw it in the used lot I knew I'd hold the picture forever.

But she'd want to know other things. I could tell her that a year ago, the Earth paused a beat to allow the news of Sputnik 1, and then began to spin even faster. I could tell her I failed to protect the girls from Elvis and his rocking hips. The most I could do was turn down the sound on Ed Sullivan. She wouldn't believe any of it, not even the secondhand TV. TV's almost had it anyway. Eddie sits beside it and thumps it with the broom handle every time the picture tube blacks out.

If I said to Maura now, "First thing you know, scientists will be putting a man on the moon," she'd say, "There's already a man on the moon. Inside. A woman, too." That would be Maura. If I told her I was worried about the children, she'd say, "The children will be just fine."

But the girls are buying boys' jeans with a fly and they're making the pant legs tight by sewing them up the inside. They think I haven't noticed, and they do their tightening when I'm not around.

"He's worried about us?" I said. "He doesn't even go to work."

"Maybe he goes certain days," said Lyd. "Where else would he be?"

"Well, I'm alone in the house all this week, so he can't be here."

Never felt right after her coffin was put to earth. The dream that night, the night I buried her, the same dream keeps coming back now. It's my past reaching through — dark light through shutters.

Last night I woke and sat up. Didn't know what to do. I'd seen her in her coffin under the earth. The coffin tilted and her head sloped to one side, lower than the rest of her body. She was trying to raise her head from the downward slant but the effort needed more energy than she had. She spoke in the dream; her eyes were sockets.

— *I'm not comfortable, Jock.*

Couldn't bear to think of her under the weight of the earth.

— *I'm not comfortable.*

Thought of going to the graveyard in the night, digging her up, levelling the coffin. Could do it even now, after all this time.

Lyd stopped reading and we looked at each other. We were both crying. She put the scribbler back beneath the sweaters and closed the mahogany drawer.

"Maybe we should tell somebody," she said.

"That we sneaked into his room and read his private journal?"

"We could tell Rebecque. We can tell her anything. Would she tell Duffy? Maybe Father talks about this stuff to Duffy."

"Elvis and his rocking hips?" I said.

But we couldn't laugh.

"Did you know he wrote stuff like this?" said Lyd. "It sounds as if he's been storing it up and now it's all pouring out."

When Father came home, Lyd and I were watching. He looked normal, but I went outside and checked around the car, not knowing what I was looking for.

"We'd better not say anything to Eddie," I told Lyd. "He'd just worry. But we have to keep an eye on Father."

After supper Father changed into his khaki shorts, checked the barometer on the porch wall and grabbed the binoculars off the sill. He drove the car to shore and parked in four inches of water on flat riverbottom. He got out, washed the car, slipped back inside and stayed there. Lyd and I went down and sat on shore with our books, pretending to study.

"Maybe he doesn't go to his office," I said. "Maybe he wanders around on this side of the river looking for work so he won't have to cross a bridge."

But he did go to work. We read the journal the next day, and the day after that. As long as he kept writing, we kept reading.

> Sat in the car and thought of water, cool under summer tires. Thought of why I can't get across the bridge without having the attacks. Thought of outwaiting rush hour, putting the car in reverse and backing across, since its nose doesn't like to be turned towards Quebec. Thought of the rattling planks on the bridge and covered the picture in my mind. Covered it the way canvas sheeting is stretched over the new car models at work when they're offloaded in secrecy before each fall unveiling.
>
> Maybe it's fear.
>
> Of the river.
>
> I should have warned Maura. Couldn't keep her safe.
>
> What I'm afraid of? I am afraid of the fear.

"Do you feel safe?" Lyd said.

"Safe?"

I remembered how Father used to warn us about the invisible line above the rapids, *the last place of safety — or not*. How I had sometimes drifted past, to see how far I could go. But that wasn't what Lyd had meant. It was too complicated to think about. And her voice was shaky.

On Thursday, Father called in sick. He'd never done that before; I couldn't remember him missing a day's work. I had the entire Chemistry text to review but he came looking for me and asked if I'd like to get some driving practice and go to Britannia, on the other side. We could take the Champlain Bridge.

But I couldn't. Chemistry was my weakest subject and my first exam.

"I thought you were sick," I said.

"Well I'm better now. And that's that."

Friday morning, Father went to work but by seven that night he hadn't come home. At seven-fifteen, he phoned.

"I'm ill," he said. "I need a drive. Come and get me. My joints are aching and my knees are weak — too weak to walk. I must have summer flu, after all."

I stomped through the field, fuming. I had to take the bus all the way from the village, had to change in Hull. By the time the two of us were in the car, it was after nine and almost dark.

"I'll sit in the back," he said. "I don't want to spread germs."

When I approached the bridge, I watched in the rearview mirror as he ducked down in the back seat. Seconds later, his head came up and he stared down at the river below. We rumbled across.

Saturday morning, Father drove to Hull to get the groceries at the A&P. No river to cross. Lyd and I made a dive for the scribbler.

Had to be bailed out by my second born, my child-between. Before I called home, tried different routes to the other bridges. No go. Had to return to glass tower and call home. Back-seat passenger in my own car. Planned to drop out of sight as soon as Trude hit the bridge. Braced for the attack and — nothing happened.

Instead, body filled with well-being. Stared at river's surface, even dared it to reach up and pull me down.

Something inside is marking time; I feel it closing in. Trude can't come to Ottawa to drive me home every night.

Barely holding myself together.

No joy.

Miss Maura. Have to let go; can't let go. Need her. Maura would know how to get me home across the bridge.

— *A broken spirit dries up the bones.*

Lyd put the scribbler back in its place. "I wish he'd sound like his old self," she said. "I wish he'd try to order us around, tell us what to do. He's never been like this before."

"It sounds as if he's sad," I told her. "I think he's losing control."

"I don't feel right," Lyd said. "Maybe we should tell him we know."

But I was against this. I was afraid Father would explode if he found out that we'd been reading his journal. It was that unstoppable journey, *Life*. Father called it "the big trip." And he'd sometimes add, "This is the happy part; this is the learning part. This is the fun part." But Father had bogged down on his journey and Lyd and I did not know what to do.

I was trying to memorize a year's work in three subjects at once and had set up a desk in the porch. Every time Lyd or Eddie walked through the house my thoughts wandered. I could hear them breathing.

I'd been trying to stay out of Father's way, too, but he seemed to be everywhere. Saturday, he'd returned from town with groceries and an armful of papers that he'd cached beside his maroon chair. I had seen him writing, pencil in hand. Scratching out, erasing, writing again. Not in the Hilroy scribbler but on long yellow foolscap. Lyd and I couldn't find the foolscap, later, but in his journal we read:

Maura and I pulled up roots in Darley against the wishes of two families. We survived years of Duplessis, the old crook. When others around me blathered on about him I knew enough to keep my mouth shut. On Saint-Jean Baptiste Day, I shook hands with the village priest — never interfered in *his* affairs and he never interfered in mine. Now Maura's gone and the priest and the "Chef" are still around. Didn't Maura follow my thumb on the map of the atlas when I hauled it down and traced the Canadian Shield? Wasn't she looking over my shoulder? No, I remember now. Behind me, she said, "You're taking me to live beside a wide river, and I don't know how to swim."

Don't know how it all went wrong. Sometimes I feel someone sit beside me on the edge of the bed

— a woman — can't see her face. I reach, but when I do, she's gone.

I dream the river running through me. I dream the river in its seasons. Shallow and log-strewn in summer, the stillness of shore-ice in winter, the turbulence of spring. Last night, I was surprised at the surface terror, the surliness of water hinting at what lies beneath. In my sleep I dreamed:

— *Maura, beneath those waves.*

— *Maura, beneath that terror.*

Woke and remembered that it was summer, not spring, when Maura drowned.

Terror, nonetheless.

In the evening, Father went to the river for his walk and I watched from the porch window. He stepped into our old rowboat, manoeuvred around some stray logs jammed in shallow water, and rowed upriver to the end of the cove. Then he turned around and rowed right back. He stood on shore looking through binoculars. I gave up and went back to my books. I did not have one speck of brain space to spare. But after school the next day, I read:

Stood on shore so I could pay attention to the view — the one I'll always call up behind my eyes. Daylight fading, checked the sky, east towards rapids, then west. Stars becoming visible. Lowered binoculars but something made me raise them again. It was early evening dusk. Have to get this down — though I don't expect to understand. Crazyman. What Maura's mother used to call me.

Crazyman. Probably still does, behind my back. Lost. I lost her daughter. Who had a darkness of her own. She would never tell me what it was but she brought it to the marriage and there was darkness between us.

This is what I saw and I will write this down. Stood on shore and found myself separate from and facing my own planet. Crazy is right. It happened so fast, I remember only the loudness of my voice as I called out to the curve of Earth.

Shouted when I recognized the outline of continents. Cried out for South America and its perfect shape. All around me, stars drifted close. Unfamiliar constellations so brilliant I couldn't have imagined. Heavens full of movement and light. One constellation stretched out, another pulled in close, shimmering with light. Tried to store what my eyes were seeing. Afraid I would not be able to recall.

Then.

Had to be asleep to see such a thing.

Above — in the sky — an egg. A giant egg, vast and luminous, tilted above Earth.

An EGG.

Must have fallen asleep.

The egg began to fade. When it shifted, I saw what it really was. A skull in the sky — an immense fleshless skull. The skull dissolved upward into the background of stars. As it disappeared — I heard Maura. As soon as I heard her voice, I knew it had always been there.

— *Protects. The caul. Protects. The caul protects.*

I called out to prove that I was awake. I WAS
NOT LYING ON THE BANK. Looked down at
my feet to see where I was. I was in the same spot,
standing at the edge of my own river.

Feet were on shale.

Shale is not Shield.

Whatever I heard and saw, I'll never speak of
again. Walked back to the house and felt like an
old old man.

It was too much. It was my turn to cook supper and I was
banging things around when Father came in. I didn't care if he
was crazy or not and I didn't care if he'd gone to work. Eddie
came in, and then Lyd. Lyd hadn't read the latest. They were
all in the kitchen.

"What are we having?" Lyd said.

"Egg," I said. "We're having E - G - G."

Father looked startled, then bewildered.

"And potatoes and a can of peas. The eggs are scrambled.
And hurry up, because after supper I have to keep on studying."

Lyd came to the porch where I was working. Father was at the
river. We could see him sitting on shore.

"I found out what was on the yellow foolscap," she said.
"Look. This is disaster. I think he's trying to advertise for a
woman. He's really upset. Everything is going wrong." She set
a double sheet from a tabloid in front of me. Clipped to it was
the yellow page in Father's printing. At the top, he'd made
rambling notes to himself:

Used to ignore these. Thought they were for the insane, the syphilitic and the needy. Now I've read column after column, and I wonder. Ads full of pleas. I'm alone, yes, but have I ever used the word *lonely*? No one else does, either. Who are the men in *Partners Wanted?* Do they sit in rooms by themselves and fill in their own descriptions? Makes me want to rage and weep at the same time. Everyone's attractive and interesting; everyone has a sense of humour, wants long walks or quiet talks or fast dancing. Or more. No matter who sends the SOS, the words are the same.

What would I write if I composed a reply, mailed it to a box number? Have never tendered an anonymous version of myself.

Widower: Loved his wife. Thinks she loved him though they hardly spoke of this to each other. (She drowned, centuries ago. Dropped off a cliff before they could get safely past middle age — Why?) Left to make decisions right or wrong, raised three children, two of them nearly grown. Wakes in a sweat at night wondering if they'll survive. Has never travelled out of the two provinces bordering the Ottawa River. Not for lack of adventure; duties more pressing. Worked in munitions, aluminum trays and cars — blundered into all three. With eyes closed, knows how to create the perfect fleur-de-lis. Sometimes dreams long pale limbs of women twined round him in the dark. As a child, memorized every poem in the Ontario red readers. Can recall and recite any stanza of "Snow Bound," not necessarily in winter. Feels like throwing in the noodle half the time. Heard wife's voice coming out of the sky one night. Did not mention this or would have been committed. Sometimes we miss the message.

"It's sex," Lyd said. "It's just damned-well sex." Sex was something she and I talked a lot about, these days. Every party we went to had "dancing in the dark," with the lights turned out. Even at the church dances, everyone seemed to be groping. Several of the girls on the basketball team at school had given photos of themselves, in skimpy nylon pyjamas, to their boyfriends. It had become a sort of secret fad.

"I don't care if it's sex or what it is," I said. "I think Father's incurable."

I was working on *Le Petit Chèvre de Monsieur Seguin,* for Oral French. After that, there was only an English exam left. I thought of using Father as the subject for my exam composition. Our teacher had told us we'd be allowed to write on any topic. I could change the names and call it fantasy. I'd already memorized the poems we'd covered during the term. With Father around I had never been unprepared for any poem thrown my way by any teacher.

Later, I told myself, later — after the exams are over — I'll sit down with Lyd and we'll figure out a plan. We'll tell Father we've read everything. We'll come clean. Then I'll leave home. He can be mad if he wants. Duffy will help him. We'll talk to Duffy and Rebecque.

Exams were finished. I had put my name in at the hospital in Ottawa and had a summer job as an assistant ward aide in the Outpatient Clinic. I was to start at the beginning of July. Lyd and Eddie and I were in the porch, feet up, telling stories. Eddie had just told us about a cave under the cliffs that he used to scrunch into when he was small enough to fit inside. Lyd and I were appalled.

"You could have fallen in," I told him. "The top of the cliff could have crumbled." I thought of him curled up in some tight spot, staring down on dark waters below. Eddie's secret.

"You sound like Father," said Eddie. "Exactly like Father."

"What would you have done if you'd fallen in?" I said. "You'd have gone right through the rapids." I didn't add that it was the very spot Mother had gone over. I didn't have to.

Father had walked to the hotel on rue Principale. He'd told us he'd check to see if Duffy was around, and he'd stay for one beer. It was almost dark and he hadn't returned. A wind was coming up across the river and from where I sat I could see clouds banked on the other side. A half-moon was barely visible in the sky. Despite the wind, the evening air was soft and warm. I felt the summer stretching out before me.

Lyd had been hired to work for the summer at Woolworth's lunch counter on Sparks Street in Ottawa. She was to start her job the following week. She still didn't know if she'd be working upstairs or down. Down was where invisible hands sent up stainless-steel bowls of egg salad, chicken salad, soft butter and cream. The bowls rose and fell on the shelves of a dumb waiter. We'd been watching them for years from twirling stools before the counter. I imagined rows of women in hair-nets, working beneath the pipes below, whipping things up for customers who ate club sandwiches and topped them off with banana splits, for dessert.

There was a commotion at the curve of our road and I stood to watch as three cars swerved past the house and turned down to the river. The cars rattled over loose stones and screeched to a halt. Someone was shouting and I looked at Lyd's face and saw that she, too, had recognized the voice of our father. The three of us tore out the screen door and down the front steps just as I saw him enter the river.

Father was fully dressed and was wading towards a snarl of logs in the cove. Never once did he glance at the main current, a few feet away. His legs seemed unsteady as his shoes stumbled from rock to rock beneath the water. I couldn't see Duffy anywhere.

Father lunged with each step and thrashed out into deeper water, always making his way upriver. I knew the bottom there, what the waters opposing him would feel like against his chest as he leaned against the force of the river. The three of us were running down to the bank but by the time we got there Father was no more than a silhouette in the dark.

He had waded to his waist and stood in one spot, now, and pulled his belt from the loops of his trousers. He snapped the belt in the air and held it taut between his hands. He leaned forward clumsily and strapped the belt to the log he'd freed from the underwater tangle. I saw him wrap his arms around the long dark shape.

"Dad!" I shouted. "Dad!"

We were yelling from shore, though the men from the cars hung back.

"*Tabernac*," I heard one of them say. "He took the bet, but he doesn't think about his children."

Father turned his face towards shore momentarily, but he was so far out I couldn't tell if he knew we were there or not. He shouted, but his words were lost in the wind.

The current was whipping at his waist and his body seemed to be learning the balance of the log as it tilted into deeper water. He stretched lengthwise, bobbed under with the log and up again in a single splash. The two shapes merged as one and floated out into the current, vanishing towards the roar. The rapids he was heading into were more than eight feet high; he was the one who knew — he'd been teaching us about them for years. Already beyond the last place of safety, he had no choice but to go straight through before he would end up *down below.*

The men on shore took to their cars on the run and headed for the split in the dirt road that would lead to the dead end below the rapids. Lyd and Eddie and I followed the short cut and raced through the Pines. I tried to glance at the river as we ran but all I could see in the dark and the moonlight were tips of white waves.

We reached the end of the old hydro wall just after the men pulled up in their cars. There was shouting as they lined up the cars, headlights beaming over water. I thought of Mimi's sister Pierrette, who'd once seen a miracle woman at the end of these rapids. I thought of Mimi and her entire family behind us and wondered if they were at the windows, staring at the commotion below.

"Damned fool," I heard.

"*Maudit.* He'll come out on wings, that one."

"Don't count on it. This English knows the water."

I saw a log toss straight up out of the whitecaps. Then

another. Eddie was between Lyd and me and I caught a glimpse of his face, tight-lipped and silent.

In the headlights, shadows darted up from the waves and flicked along the surface of the river. Every one of us knew that Father had to be through the rapids by now. He would have been through before we'd reached the Pines. Even so, we stood there waiting.

And then, I thought of something else. How the water swirled to shore and even seemed to change direction farther down, close to the edge of another protected cove. Bodies were found in the bottomless place beneath the booms between here and there, but what about someone who'd gone past, someone who'd survived?

I made a dash for the path and ran farther down. And heard the rasp of my father, a soaked wet rasp to my right. He was striding through the waves, shedding sheets of water as he crossed the width of the lower cove and made his way back upriver. His belt was gone and his trousers torn. He staggered in the shallow water — and he fell. I thought I heard him curse as he went down but I wasn't sure. I was in the river, shouting, when he hit the rocks, in water not even as high as his ankles.

I tried to drag him to shore but he shook me off, saying there wasn't a thing wrong with him. He'd shot the rapids on a log and had come through alive. But he'd cracked his knee against a sharp rock when he'd fallen, and now he couldn't get up.

"Damn you — damn you!" I yelled. "What are you trying to do? We were so scared. You should see Eddie's face. He's terrified. What's the matter with you? Are you crazy? Don't you know Mother drowned? Why are you trying to kill yourself?"

He looked up for a moment as if he couldn't think what to

reply. And then, to my surprise, he rested his cheek back in the water as if he might stay there and sleep.

"I'm not trying to kill myself," he said out of the side of his mouth. "I'm not. I had to know if it was the fear."

I was soaked now, too, but refused to get into the car when a man on each side helped Father limp over so they could drive him home. Lyd sat with him on the back seat. Eddie and I ran home the same way we'd come, through the Pines. I kept thinking of Lyd's face when she'd climbed in beside Father. She had looked as old as Granny Tracks.

I wanted to reach home at the same time as the cars but when we got to the cliff Eddie began to cry. He slowed down and sobbed and sobbed as I'd never heard anyone sob, and he would not, or could not, stop.

"Please, Eddie," I said. "Stop crying. He didn't drown. It was a stupid thing, that's all. He was proving something to himself. Something about Mother. He didn't drown, Eddie. He didn't drown."

"He *couldn't* drown!" Eddie yelled at me. He was mad and he was crying so hard his chest was heaving with hiccups. "He couldn't drown, because of the caul!" he shouted. "It's in the name book. If you're born with the caul, you *can't* drown. Didn't you see what was written in the Bible Uncle Ewart gave us?"

"What are you talking about?"

He wouldn't stop crying and kept spluttering between sobs. "It's in the name book. Mother's old name book. I looked up *caul* at the beginning to see what it means."

But he would not stop crying.

Father was dragging his leg across the living room when we returned to the house. The men were gone; the cars had roared back to the hotel. Lyd was behind Father, two feet behind, her arms stretched out towards him. And he fell a second time, just as Eddie and I entered the room. He collapsed in front of the long mirror, his face holding surprise, as if it had not known the presence of his legs when his body went down. The three of us leaned towards him, Eddie crying so hard the sound filled the entire house. Father tried to straighten but could only push himself as far as his hands and knees. He stayed that way, staring into the mirror that had once belonged to Duffy's runaway wife.

He seemed astonished to see his own white face at knee level. Eye stared into eye. Ignoring the reflection of the three of us behind, Father spoke — it was impossible to say whether to us or to himself. "This . . ." he said, and I remembered later that his voice had held not a trace of self-pity.

"This . . . is the suffering part."

MOVING ON

LEANING, LEANING
OVER WATER

1959

Father's knee had to be repaired in two stages and between operations he moved us out of Quebec. Most of his English friends had already left. Only Duffy remained. He would stick it out, he told Father, even though prosperity was across the river.

I had taken my driver's test and did most of the driving now, because Father was in an above-the-knee cast. It wasn't the first time he'd been in a cast and he was able to get around, but driving he could not do. Duffy and Rebecque helped us with the many trips to move the small things and after that we hired a man with a truck. Father had found a house in Ottawa South. From our windows there was no view of a river.

We left the piano behind for Rebecque. She and Duffy were moving into our house, which Duffy was buying back from

185

Father. Rebecque had begun to take piano lessons and loved to sit grandly before the old Heintzman, her hands sweeping the keys, searching out their deep rich tones.

Before we left, Father stood in the empty living room and looked at me. "You've missed your calling," he said, and closed the lid over the keyboard of my piano. I thought of him standing behind me, bleating out "The Whiffenpoof," and I was not sorry. I had not missed my calling; I did not know what my calling was.

When I went to Mimi's house to say goodbye, Mimi was filled with an excitement of her own. The bus she took from work every day to get home to St. Pierre had added a new route, a diversion down a long treed road that led to the Hull jail. She had peered into the barred windows, she said, every time the bus turned into the loop, trying to get a look at a prisoner, even though she knew now that the cells were at the back. The guards who worked at the jail took the bus at their change of shift. Several months ago, one of them, Rosaire, had begun to sit with her at the back of the bus. They'd been going out ever since. This weekend they were going to a club in Gatineau to hear western music.

We hugged and I wondered if we'd see each other after I moved away. I rarely bumped into her now.

Mimi shrugged. "Us," she said, "we'll never move." She swept her hands up and out, to encompass the whole big family house.

I had started my own work at the Ottawa hospital, where Father's second knee operation was scheduled. I had not told Father I was leaving. I was tempted to go back to school because, in Ontario, I would be placed in grade thirteen, skipping a whole year. But I had finished high school in Quebec, and had made up my mind. Eddie would be entering grade seven, the same as if he'd stayed in Quebec. Already, he had met a boy his age on our street. Lyd had the summer to work at Woolworth's before she returned for her second year at the business school.

My job had begun on a Monday morning. I walked to the end of the block and took a streetcar to the hospital. There I joined a stream of workers as they entered the staff entrance, a side door that led to a basement hall lined with lockers. At five minutes to eight I was given a blue-and-white smock to put on and told to follow a man who was wearing grey overalls and a grey shirt, with a grey badge on his sleeve. He led me in silence through a maze of corridors and stairs, up to the main floor, beyond the swinging doors of Emergency. We crossed a bright open room that was filled with rows of wooden seats not unlike the pews in Union Station. These pews were filled, not with travellers, but with the comings and goings of the ailing population of Ottawa.

I was trying to stay close to the man in grey. He hadn't said one word or acknowledged me in any way. As I walked between two central pews, a man in a worn brown suit reached for me and called out, "Help me, nurse. For God's sake, stop and help me." I kept my head down and pretended not to hear in case blood started pouring out of him. This was a hospital, after all.

I was suddenly brought face to face with Emmy Lusk, chief ward aide of the Outpatient Clinic. The overalled man turned on one heel and retreated around the corner.

"Don't mind him," said Emmy Lusk. "He never talks to anybody. He's one brick short of a load. So you're my summer student." She did not pause for breath. "You're s'posed to follow me around. Fat chance you'd get a real orientation. They make sure we're shorthanded, they even intend it. When we get a student, we're s'posed to be grateful. But what they pay keeps us so broke we couldn't buy a pair of leggings for a hummingbird. Your pay's even less," she said, and jabbed me in the arm with one finger.

On two sides of the room, lab-coated men were moving from one examining area to another, each space divided from the next by beige curtains hung from a network of tracks that criss-crossed the ceiling. Because the curtains hung well above the floor, I could see knees — countless bare feet and knees. All manner of legs. On the fourth side of the room, traffic flowed towards and away from the nurses' station. There were three examining rooms beyond that and, at the end, two elevators.

Emmy Lusk pointed to her smock of solid blue, telling me that the aides were one level below orderlies, who wore white. She told me that the patients in the pews couldn't tell one outfit from another. "They think we're all nurses and doctors," she said. "You have to get used to it." I thought of the man in the brown suit but did not tell Emmy that he'd cried out for help when I'd passed.

"Let's go," she said abruptly — everything about her was abrupt. She barged through a door and I followed her into a padded freight elevator that took us up to the fourth floor.

"This is where we do the juice cart," she announced, and she led me into a long kitchen. "Trud-ee," she said, reading my name tag. "Is that how you say it?"

"Trude," I told her. "It rhymes with rude."

"Is that so?" she said. "Well, *Trood,* your first job is to prepare the cart. Up here is where we load and unload the tins. We make the eggnog, break six eggs, add two good dashes of vanilla." As she spoke, her hands cracked eggs, tossed the shells, pressed buttons for whirring blades, filled stainless jugs with unnatural-looking green lemonade, and with milk from the cow. The cow was divided down its stainless steel middle into skim and whole. The milk poured out through stiff rubber tubes that hung from its bottom.

"Elvis calls these the titties," said Emmy, watching my face. "Elvis is the orderly up here. He does both sides, four east and west. You've got to watch your step, he's twice your age. He can charm the skin off a snake. He's got sideburns, too. Like real Elvis."

But Elvis did not show his face all morning.

We jiggled the loaded cart onto the elevator and went back down to Outpatient, where the pew population had already changed. The man in the brown suit had vanished. I looked towards the beige curtains. Maybe he'd had to drop his drawers; maybe two of the bare legs I could see belonged to him. If so, I didn't want to know.

Emmy and I took turns wheeling the cart between pews, dispensing prune juice and lemonade, pouring water, scooping ice chips into paper cups.

"Push the eggnog," Emmy told me. "Holler it right out. We have to get rid of it all. If the patients are old, they need the prune, that's a fact. The ones that don't look constipated, they get the nog. The ones that aren't old and have a tight look, they get the prune, too."

I spent the next two hours searching out Ottawa's constipated, row by row. Just before I was ready to go back upstairs, a patient stopped me near the nurses' station and placed a jar in my hand.

"Tapeworm," he said. "All in one piece." He was immensely pleased with himself. "Doc told me I should try to catch it and bring the fellar in. Would you give it to the Doc?"

I looked at the greyness of ribboned segments in the jar and felt a long slow gag roll over the back of my tongue. Emmy swept in beside me and plucked the jar from my hand.

"Nurses' business," she said, and shooed the man back to his pew. She banged the jar onto the countertop that barricaded the nurses from three sides.

"Come on," she said. "We only have thirty minutes and we're on early lunch. You'll get to meet Elvis this time, for sure."

"One afternoon," Elvis said, looking directly into my face, "I had a call to bring a stretcher from the autopsy room to the lab on eleven. Research, they said. When I got there, you might say I was curious about the lumps and bumps under the sheet." He crammed a cigarette into the side of his mouth and held the flame while he talked. "I waited till I was inside the elevator." He stopped and dragged. "I thought, Why not, why not take a look."

I could tell that Emmy had heard this story before. She was glancing around the cafeteria, raising a hand to greet the other ward aides, all in their solid blues. The aides and orderlies ate in a roped-off section of their own. There was an ashtray on each table and everyone was dragging and puffing. Elvis inhaled deeply but the smoke didn't come back out of him. I watched his lips, his nostrils, even his ears, to see where it might be released.

"So I go to the end of the stretcher and lift a corner of the sheet," he said. "Turn it back and find that I'm keeping company with a stretcher of human heads."

"Lookit that Mayberry tart," said Emmy. "She's been up all night again. Her eyes look like two pee-holes in the snow. You'd think she'd be ashamed."

"Human heads," said Elvis, and a rush of smoke exited his body. "Do you think they were propped on their necks like mannequin heads? No. Each head was lying in a basin, staring up."

"He makes half of it up," said Emmy. "Don't pay any attention. I've heard this story before — the lab needed the heads to get the stuff out of the glands, the *pitchootaries*. I asked one of the nurses. Come on, girl, back we go. The pews will be full up again, after lunch."

"Come and see me on four, Trude-the-rude," Elvis said. "I'll show you my shortcut through the back halls."

"Told you," said Emmy. "Smooth as satin on a bedpost. Doesn't take long and you learn to ignore him."

I went straight to Woolworth's after my shift. I was exhausted. I found Lyd at the far end of the store, mopping the countertop. There were four empty stools in her section so she had a few minutes to talk. She brought me a heavy pedestalled glass filled with ice chips and ginger ale and I sipped slowly through a straw.

Lyd had to wear a cotton cap that she hated; it was the colour of apricots. And a short-sleeved blouse to match, identical to those worn by every other waitress behind the counter, and a pull-over apron, buttoned down the back. Against her height, the apron looked as if it had been hoisted up and stuck to her lap. Every time I saw her I wanted to laugh.

"If you laugh," she said, "I'll kill you."

"You should see what I have to wear at the hospital," I

said, though I didn't mind the smock. At least I didn't have to wear anything on my head.

I began to tell Lyd about the tapeworm but she gave me a warning signal. None of her co-workers knew that I was her sister, and we didn't let on.

A middle-aged couple and an elderly woman had approached. The old woman was short and birdlike and had henna hair that stuck straight out of the back of her head. The man and woman hoisted her, one on each side, until she was seated safely between them. I wondered if she'd fall off the stool; its base was on a raised platform and she'd had to step high to reach that. It was hard to tell if the three were related, or if the couple were even man and wife. They seemed to be on an outing, and though I tried not to stare, I sat there and listened to every word.

Lyd brought their orders — hot beef sandwiches with peas and gravy and chips for the couple, and mashed potatoes with crinkly skinned chicken for the old woman. After only one spoonful of potatoes, the old woman cried out, "I'm FULL, I'm FULL!" Her words were slurred, as if her teeth had clamped over them. Lyd was taken by surprise and turned quickly, her wrist knocking a breadboard to the floor. I tried not to look at her. The old woman shouted again, "I'm FULL," as if the others were forcibly stuffing her.

The man kept on eating, not giving her a sideways glance.

"You poured honey in my shoes," the old woman accused, pointing at him. "You know that perfectly well."

Lyd had bolted to the end of the counter. I slid off the stool and followed, on the opposite side. She was exhausted, too, I could tell, but she held down her laughter. I wanted to tell her about the hospital but there wasn't time.

"They didn't tell us about this," she said.

"Who?"

"Mother and Father," she said. "They never told us what was out here, in the world."

One morning after I'd handed out the juices, Emmy swooped to my side. "You're wanted on four," she said. "They're short up there and going out flat. They need a student to sit with a patient. Don't worry, you'll be back in an hour or so. Sometimes the wards call for extra help, they've done it before."

On the fourth floor the patients were wearing white johnny shirts instead of their own street clothes as they did in Outpatient. A nurse was waiting for me at the desk and took me down the hall and into a single room. I did not know how to tell her that I'd never been in a patient's room. I didn't know what to say.

"Sit there, on the chair," she said. "We're short-handed till we get everyone through their lunch breaks. Every time Mr. Leeson tries to get out of bed you stand at the rails and tell him you mean business. We mean business, don't we, Mr. Leeson! You're not going to climb over that bar again, are you! You're not going to hurt yourself. Remember when you fell on the floor, Mr. Leeson?"

He would not acknowledge her, and she turned and left the room. He had thick soft-looking white hair and looked as ordinary as anyone could look. He was propped against three pillows. A voice from the end of the hall shouted, "Get the baby, damn you," and a few seconds later, "Get the baby!"

Mr. Leeson eyed me from afar.

"You see how impossible it is," he said. He spoke as if this were a continuing conversation between us. "It's impossible to get any rest when the old and the dying shout obscenities all day and all night long. Obscenities pool in our brains." He spoke kindly, as if he might be someone's grandfather. "Obscenities dribble out of us in our old age. Also other bodily fluids — an unstoppable flow." He closed his eyes and seemed to fall asleep, although one eyelid was partly open.

I was sorry for him, for the way the nurse had spoken. I thought of Grampa King in his navy suit in the coffin, how unnatural he'd looked when he was not in overalls. I relaxed, for a second.

Mr. Leeson was up and over the end of the bed, sliding backwards, headfirst and down. I caught him before he hit the floor but his head was resting on my shoes. He was too heavy to hoist and the bell was too far to reach, so I had to shout. He was hanging by his feet, which were caught in a tangle of blankets and the end rail. His knees were bent and he was upside down, pyjama bottoms askew, johnny shirt dragging, mouth open, his white hair electrified and brushing the floor. Elvis and the nurse came running in.

"We'll have to tie him again," the nurse said to Elvis. She spoke as if I were not present. "Go and get the straitjacket from the linen cart."

They hauled Mr. Leeson to an upright position and leaned him back into the pillows. He glared at me as if I'd betrayed him. When the straitjacket was brought he slipped into it passively. He did not object when it was laced up the back or when his arms were inserted into absurdly long sleeves. He did not object when the sleeves were crossed and tied to opposite bed rails. He looked like an ancient and bony bird, its wings folded recklessly. I thought of Granny Tracks, who often said, "Much flapping breaks wings."

"You have to learn, Trude-the-rude," said Elvis. "You have to learn that when you're with a patient, *you're* in charge."

I looked at him and was almost grateful. But I was Mr. Leeson's betrayer. I had not kept him safe. I was sent back to Outpatient and spent the afternoon helping Emmy in the examining rooms, replenishing supplies.

Every night, in our new home, Father asked how we liked our jobs, and Lyd and I said, "Fine." We didn't tell him the details, though we told each other — every one. I had begun to understand that the hospital was a place like no other. It was like a city within many walls. It had a population, contained. Every day held the adventures of intimate lives and, every day, there was a tallying of stories. Stories were told around the nurses' desk and at coffee break and in the lunchroom and beside the basement lockers. Doctors, nurses, lab technicians, orderlies, ward aides, clerks and housekeeping staff all exchanged stories. Patients told them to one another while they waited in the pews, and they told them to the cleaning staff who were sympathetic, and they told them to me. Elvis continued to tell his stories and Emmy kept up a running account by my side. There was never a morning or an afternoon when a story was not told. I listened to them all. It was as if each person were recounting a life up to the point of the telling. Bringing the self forward to each new day. I had never heard so many stories.

While these stories were multiplying, our own stories at home had slowed down. The Hilroy scribbler had disappeared with the move. Father had gone back to work for the car dealer, in his cast, and did not seem to be doing strange things.

Nor did he ever speak of or brag about shooting the rapids, though, when I considered the act, I thought it amazing. The second stage of his knee surgery was coming up and I was watching for the right moment to tell him I was leaving. He thought I'd be going back to school in September. I wasn't making much money at the hospital but it was enough for my trainfare west and to get started.

Throughout the summer, Elvis kept up his banter, trying to shock, always trying to make me react. One day in the cafeteria he told me that a friend of his had taken a girlfriend swimming in the Ottawa River and they had "done it" underwater.

"After they finished, they couldn't separate," he said. "They had to be pried apart."

"My God," said Emmy. "Are you ever going to let up?"

I wasn't worried about Elvis. I could see through him and, anyway, Emmy was there as a buffer. I never knew what she was going to say, but I'd learned that she had taken it upon herself to look after me.

I told Lyd about the swimmers when I was leaning into the counter at Woolworth's.

"Nobody around here tells stories like that," she said. "It's a joke. Surely it can't be true."

She and I went to the "Y" dances on Metcalfe Street every Saturday night, now that we lived in the city. Lyd was going out with a student at the university. I had met a boy named Ross at a "Y" dance and twice we'd been to the movies. I couldn't imagine telling him any of the Elvis stories. I couldn't imagine telling them to anyone, except to Lyd.

Father's knee repair was scheduled for a Thursday afternoon. He was admitted to the ninth floor on Wednesday night to be prepared for surgery and I had driven his car to the hospital Thursday morning so I could pick up Lyd and bring her to the ward. We planned to be in his room when he was brought back upstairs from the Recovery Room.

Thursday was also gynecology day at the clinic.

"G-Y-N day," Emmy said in the morning, spelling out the word as everyone did.

"G-Y-N day today," said a nurse. "All women." She made a face. The pews were filled with women of all ages, from girls in their teens to the very old.

Occasionally, because the Outpatient Clinic was next to Emergency, a patient was wheeled in on a stretcher when the Emergency Room was full. I was sometimes asked to stand beside someone while the nurses and doctors caught up on the backload of priority cases.

"Just press the wall buzzer if there's a problem," the head nurse told me. "Someone will come running."

Two of our three examining rooms were full when I was asked to go into the middle room and stay with a forty-year-old woman who had been spotting in the middle of a late pregnancy. Emmy rolled her eyes. We were giving out the afternoon juices and the pews were full. We'd been running since early morning.

I was worried about the responsibility but I also knew that there were so many people in our clinic I could open the door and yell if I needed someone. Because it was G-Y-N day, the woman's doctor was in the clinic anyway; he was with another patient.

The woman smiled at me when I went in and then she closed her eyes. She was wearing a johnny shirt and was tucked up to her chin in a heap of blankets. Even so, she kept shuddering. The walls of the examining rooms were thin and we could hear her doctor in the next room, questioning a patient.

The woman behind the wall did not seem to understand English; a second woman was translating.

"My mother doesn't want surgery," said the voice.

"Well, her uterus is falling out," the doctor's voice said. "Tell her." He seemed exasperated. "I've inserted a pessary. What happens when she has sex?"

"Ma?" said the younger voice, and a flurry of words was exchanged between the two. I didn't know the language; it wasn't French.

"She says my father is rough," said the voice.

"She has to tell him not to be rough, or I'm going to have to operate."

There was a long excited conversation between mother and daughter.

"She says my father isn't going to like it," said the young woman's voice.

My patient opened her eyes and moved her head back and forth as if to say, "For God's sake, do we have to listen to this woman's private life?" But there was nothing we could do to escape. We heard the door shut on silence and then our own door opened. The doctor came in and I fled.

I headed for Emmy who was across the room but the head nurse intercepted. "I'm sorry, Trude, we're getting another patient from Emergency. I don't know what's going on over there but we can't staff our own clinic and look after *their* patients, too. I don't have a nurse or a pair of hands to spare.

If you'll stand beside the new patient in room three, I'll have her prepped for surgery as soon as someone's free."

Emmy was beckoning with one hand and shaking her head back and forth but I had no choice.

"It's a young woman," the nurse went on. "She's stable now, apparently. I don't have her name yet — she's to go straight to the OR from here. Just a kid, I guess. Abortion. She stuck knitting needles up herself. Jesus." She shook her head. "Jesus, Jesus."

I went into room three and shoved chairs out of the way. An orderly was pushing a stretcher towards me from the swinging doors. A young woman, small-boned, her face as white as parchment, was wheeled in.

"Mimi?" I said. "Mimi, oh God."

Mimi lifted a hand out from under the blankets and reached for one of mine. Her fingers were cold; I could feel the bones of them under her skin.

The orderly and I lifted and pushed her over to the examining table. He rolled up the bloody sheets and stuffed them onto the lower shelf of his stretcher and wheeled it back towards his own department. "Watch her, kid," he called over his shoulder, and he shut the door.

"I really did it this time," Mimi said. "I'm so scared."

She reached for my hand again and gripped me as if she would be cast adrift if she were to let go. Streaks had appeared on her face as if someone had pressed long hard fingers into her cheeks. Even so, she seemed to be gathering herself fiercely.

"I think I was bleeding a lot," she said. "It feels like it stopped now." She twisted herself to her side and faced the wall as if she didn't want to see me any more. "I guess you and I never thought we'd be here," she said. "I really have something to tell the priest at confession, now."

I felt an edge, a twist to her voice. She flopped onto her back suddenly and looked scared again.

"Get something quick, Trude. It's coming." She yanked at and kicked the blankets away from her and I reached for the buzzer.

"No!" she said. "Put something under me. Quick."

I looked between her legs and what I saw first were two tiny feet. They were the colour of red rubber erasers and were hanging out of her. Then, membranous knees and perfect miniature legs, the whole tiny body emerging from Mimi feet-first like some bad voodoo joke, veins and arteries attached on the outside.

I reached to the shelf for the first thing I could grab and shoved a basin between Mimi's legs. The baby slipped into it and lay there, its rubbery body coiled into permanence against the cool silver sides. It was about seven inches long. A complete human being. A dead and still and purply red minia-ture being with sealed eyes like membranes, and a tiny penis, and fingers and toes all separate and complete. It might have washed up on a shore of some remote and bloody river, the name of which we had never known.

I pressed the buzzer on the wall and heard Mimi at the head of the mattress, a new hardened Mimi in a new hardened voice, staring up at the ceiling, saying, just as blood began to pool and the door opened and a nurse ran in: "Is it out yet? Did you get it all out?"

I drove to Woolworth's to get Lyd and thought about Father. I'd gone upstairs to the surgical floor during my lunch break. He'd been wearing a hospital robe and was standing at the window looking down over Ottawa's streets. I knew he hated traffic, did not like being in the city, did not want the suffocation of its throb and beat around him. I knew, also, that now that he was free of St. Pierre, he'd never go back. He had told me once that what a man wanted was a house he could drive up to. Where he could park his car at the curb and know that his family was safe, inside. Where he could walk down the street and be greeted occasionally by a handshake and the warm touch of an old friend.

His surgery was scheduled for the end of the day, the last case in Orthopedics. I told him I'd be picking up Lyd, that we'd be in the room when he returned to his ward. Eddie had an evening paper route in our area and would meet us later, at the hospital.

"This isn't much," Father said. He made a gesture towards his knee. "They have to take out the pin, make sure the joint's okay, that's all." He seemed to be preparing himself. I knew he was glad that Lyd and I would be there, later.

I drove downtown and parked on O'Connor. It wasn't Father I was worried about now — he was okay. It was Mimi's face that was in front of me. She had tried to grin — weakly — when I'd left the examining room. She'd been wheeled to the operating room shortly after that. Emmy had figured out that Mimi was my friend. At coffee break, even Elvis had been quiet. Warned, probably.

I began to think about the time Bee-Bee had tied us up, Mimi and me, upstairs in their big house. I'd been nine years old, turned ten that summer. Mimi and I had never talked about the incident, after that night. But I'd never forgotten what Bee-Bee's face had looked like when he'd stood over us in the shadows, and when he'd leaned, slack-jawed, into the closet door. I wondered what Mimi would do now — if she would go back to being a filing clerk, and if she and Rosaire, the guard from the jail, would keep going out. The look on Mimi's face stayed before me: she'd seemed so small. And the way she'd gathered herself. Some part of her had already moved on.

Lyd pushed out through the back door of Woolworth's and I watched as she made her way along the street. She walked the way Mother used to walk; her hair was pinned up neatly and she glanced side to side as she came towards the car. I could imagine Lyd living here forever, being content to stay in one city the rest of her life. I was glad that we were friends and that I loved her as much as I did, but I knew that I would never be like her and settle for the same things.

"Another one of those days," she said as she got in. "I'll never eat another western sandwich as long as I live. She sniffed the sleeve of her cardigan. "I smell like oil," she said. "I smell like something fried. I smell like mayonnaise and bacon."

I pointed the car towards LeBreton Flats. I had no plan; I suddenly knew where I wanted to be.

"You look like a ghost," she said. "Where are we going? Isn't the hospital back there?"

"We have time," I said. "Father won't even be in Recovery till around five." I spoke as if I knew how everything worked at the hospital. I heard it in my own voice.

Lyd settled back. "Surprise me," she said. "The river?"

I didn't answer. I drove across the Chaudière Bridge and through Hull and cut down to the lower road. I could see glints of blue through leaves on the left. We passed the golf courses and the old car barns. I drove for twenty minutes and parked Father's car in front of our old house on Brébeuf; I knew Duffy and Rebecque would be at work. I headed for the edge of the river and Lyd fell into silence beside me, at the cove.

The water was low, and rocks were exposed here and there along the riverbed. Two logs side by side on a rock shelf were drying in the sun. There was a breeze and I tilted my face into it so I could feel it on my skin. The woods to the right of the cove were the same as they'd always been, a line of trees into which purple martins lowered themselves in quick vanishing clouds every summer evening at dusk. Mother had loved the purple martins.

Lyd and I began to walk downriver, following the bank close to the edge. Past the deceptively still shallows we'd often waded through, bare foot, bracing ourselves, feet apart on sharp-edged bottom. I thought about how, as children, we'd stood in water close to shore, bending forward over the soft grey waves in front of the house. Mother had stood in the river beside us, washing her own and our hair. Soap bubbles swirled around our thighs, were caught by the current, streaked away towards the rapids. She'd helped us rinse once, twice, taking turns. Dipped our heads into the river until each strand squeaked between forefinger and thumb. When we finished rinsing we waded the few steps to shore and bent forward again while Mother opened the towels and wrapped our hair. Gently tilting our heads back, creating a turban with a firm twist of her wrist. "There," she said. I could hear her voice, even now. "Run up to the house and dry. Sit out in the sun while you brush."

Lyd and I kept walking, making our way along the banks of shale until we were forced to higher ground. When we entered the Pines we still hadn't spoken. I glanced to the left, towards the bushes where we'd crouched to watch Mother in the light of the bonfire. It was the last time we'd seen her alive, the night of the corn roast. It was the same place I'd stood on the cliff and tried to fix my gaze on the tip of a wave, a single spot. A childhood game I was sure I would grow to conquer. After Mother drowned I had tried, over and over, to imagine the exact place her life had been swept away. If only I could know that one spot, I had told myself — but the thought was never complete. The spot had been impossible to hold. The eyes shifted with the current, jerked back, would never stay still.

"I used to think," I said to Lyd, "every time I came up here — after Mother — every time I walked here I used to say to myself: *You have to get past the clump of bushes where you and Lyd hid. Keep on. You have to get past.*"

"You, too?" said Lyd.

"Our mother jumped off the cliff," I said. I was astonished at what I heard my voice say.

I felt Lyd's body tighten, beside me. "Oh, Trude," she said, "my God, don't say that."

"She might have," I said.

"We don't *know* that. We couldn't possibly know that."

"We've never *said* that," I said.

"Well, maybe she didn't."

"She was saying something, that night by the fire. I always wished I could have known." I looked at Lyd's face and then out across the river. "She did or she didn't. We'll never know."

"Look at us," said Lyd. "Since she died. We've been trying to recover our balance, every one. Father. You and I. Eddie. That's what it comes down to."

"We never talked about this before," I said.

"There was nothing to say," she said. We were both silent.

I remembered how we'd walked in the river when we were younger. Farther up, beyond the house. Sometimes we'd be wearing shorts in the water, or underpants. The current was swift but from the beginning we seemed to know how to make our way. Chest level, arms outstretched at our sides, horse-shoe ripples forming around our bodies as we leaned over the surface of the water and thrust ourselves one step, another and another. Recovering and recovering and recovering. Always having to regain balance before the next step, catch-ing the rhythm that would keep us moving against current until either the water was too deep, or until we fatigued and had to dog-paddle back, or let the current sweep us down until the skin of our legs scraped bottom. Then, back to the starting point again. I knew that Lyd was right.

Ahead of us now, I could see iron spikes twisting up out of the ruins. We stopped abruptly and stared into a gap of about thirty feet. A chunk of wall was down, a huge chunk.

The wide ledge from which Eddie and I had tossed worms pressed to hooks was gone. The section upon which Mimi and I had sat staring down into rapids was gone. Fallen into fast water. Three massive sections now lay in the rapids where waves were rushing around their angular concrete shapes. One enormous chunk, dull and mottled, rested on its side, a blanket wave smooth across its surface. The bank, a gaping mixture of loose dirt and embedded rock, was laid bare as if the huge mass had skidded down on its way to whirlpools below. Water swirled as it gathered, rippled and broke into smaller eddies. The colour had changed; new light splashed over new surfaces. There was movement, continuous move-ment. That was all. Water spilling from one shelf to another and another, joining in steady downward flow. What remained of the wall — no longer an unbroken line — tilted heavily over rapids.

The path came to an end. There was nothing more to see. Only *down below.* I thought of Mimi's house at the end of the rapids. I thought of Mimi's weak grin as she had been wheeled away. I knew I would never tell Lyd about holding the basin between Mimi's legs. It was another secret to be kept inside while all of us, separately and together, were trying to make our way.

"We have to tell Father," Lyd said. "About the wall. He always said it would fall."

But it didn't matter to me now.

"Look," said Lyd. "The water's so clear, I can see my reflection."

I leaned forward and looked down and, as I did, I felt the sound, the roar of rapids, as it took hold inside my head. I knew that I would not be back here for a long time.

"I don't know," I said. "There are shadows." And I thought: Sometimes we see our reflection, sometimes we don't. It depends on how dark is the sky.